MW01120933

DARTMOUTH REGIONAL LIBRARY

Evelyn M. Richardson

Ben Peach and the Pirates

Ben Peach
and the
Pirates

Evelyn M. Richardson

NIMBUS
PUBLISHING LTD

Copyright © 1991 by Anne Wickens and Elizabeth June Smith

All rights reserved. No part of this publication may be reproduced or transmitted in any form or by any means electronic or mechanical, including photocopying, recording, or any information storage and retrieval system without the prior written permission of the publisher. Any request for photocopying, recording, taping or information storage and retrieval systems of any part of this book shall be directed in writing to the Canadian Reprography Collective, 379 Adelaide Street, West, Suite M1, Toronto, Ontario, M5V 1S5.

Nimbus Publishing Limited
P.O. Box 9301, Station A
Halifax, N.S.
B3K 5N5

Design Editor: Kathy Kaulbach
Project Editor: Alexa Thompson
Cover Illustration: Kathy Kaulbach
Photo: Bob Brooks

Note: The author's original text has been edited, and several sentences and paragraphs are not as originally composed by E.M. Richardson.

Nimbus Publishing Limited gratefully acknowledges the support of the Maritime Council of Premiers and the Department of Communications.

Canadian Cataloguing in Publication Data

Richardson, Evelyn M. (Evelyn May), 1902-1976.

Ben Peach and the pirates
(Newwaves)
ISBN 1-55109-031-7

I. Title. II. Series.
PS8535.I32B46 1992   jC813'.54   C92-098696-X
PZ7.R52Be 1992

Printed and bound in Canada

Contents

Foreword

Since Nova Scotia is almost an island, inhabitants have always turned to the surrounding sea. By 1840, when the events of this story took place, the blunt bows of its homemade wooden ships were pushing across the seven seas. Many of the crew were dying of foreign fevers, or going down with the ships lost in tropical hurricanes and Atlantic gales. Yet salt winds and billowing sails never ceased to lure boys from every part of the province.

Many of the smaller vessels sailed with lumber and fish for the West Indies and brought back cargoes of rum, sugar and molasses. This is the true story about the crew of one of these staunch little craft and their encounter with danger worse than the usual disease and storm—attack by pirates.

Young Ben Peach of Liverpool, Nova Scoita, played a leading part in the cruel adventure, and his account of it has come down to us. It is supported by an official letter from the British Consul in Havana, Cuba, and by newspapers of the day. I have not been able to find Ben's birth date, but as that hard life meant early retirement, and since he was still going to sea in the 1880s, and since many boys started seafaring before their teens, I have made him a lad of fifteen in 1840.

I have borrowed background details from the logs and journals kept on other vessels making West Indian voyages during the period of Ben's ill-fated cruise.

Evelyn M. Richardson

1
Outward Bound

I was a happy boy on that frosty March morning in 1840 when I set sail from Halifax on my first long voyage. Three months later, when I returned, I had proved myself a man.

Back home in the little port of Liverpool, my mother had often told me, "You have your father's blue eyes, Ben, and his quick smile." I was always pleased to hear her say this, for I had loved my father and been proud of him. Yet, when I teased my two little sisters beyond their endurance, they could fling at me, "Freckle-face" and "Snub-nose"—certain of hitting the mark.

I might have nothing to brag about in the way of looks (being mostly elbows and knees and big hands) but I was strong and sure-footed about decks and rigging. Barely fifteen, I knew I still had some growing to do but—what really counted, since I had become "the man of the family" when my father was lost at sea—I was now big enough to fill a seaman's berth on the brigantine *Vernon*, bound for Cienfuegos, Cuba.

On our morning of departure, rotting fragments of winter ice-cakes were bobbing under the Halifax wharf where the *Vernon* lay at her loading berth. Her stubby bowsprit formed a branch in the dense forest of bowsprits that dripped long shadows across the wharf-planks. The last of her cargo had been stowed, and she was waiting only for the turn of the early tide.

I sniffed the pleasant scents of teas and spices floating to me from the English square-rigger that pressed close on the *Vernon's* starboard. The stronger odor of salt cod came from the Newfoundland schooner nudging our larboard planks. All about me rose the confused shouts, creaks, rattles and thumps of the busy waterfront, as cargoes were stowed or unloaded.

Like any good mate, Mr. MacLeod was everywhere about the *Vernon's* deck, giving final inspection to rigging and gear, making sure that all was shipshape before putting to sea. John MacLeod was our next-door neighbor in Liverpool, and I hoped I would grow up to be a man like him. Ashore, between voyages, he was head carpenter at the shipyard, sang bass in our church choir and was known as a kind husband and father. At sea he was a master's mate, respected and liked by the crews under him.

"Belay that starb'd halyard there, Ben!" he called. Eager to show him my skill as a seaman, I hastened to make fast the loose rope he indicated.

On the *Vernon's* afterdeck, Mr. Strachan was having a last discussion with Captain Cunningham. Mr. Strachan was the Halifax merchant who had chartered the *Vernon* to carry a cargo of dried and barrelled fish to Cuba. Despite his beaver hat and fur-lined coat, he looked chilled, but he called a warm, "Good day, Cap'n," as he swung over the rail to the wharf. I was glad he hadn't wished us "Fair winds" or "God speed" as landsmen sometimes do. Like most seamen, I believed such farewells brought bad luck to a ship.

Captain Cunningham nodded a friendly reply. Then, with a glance about the deck, he went below to his cabin. I was much in awe of our quiet captain—a tall thin man, with more salt than pepper in his beard. He had a firm mouth and keen blue eyes, yet his face often held a faraway, weary look.

I turned to George MacKay, our ship's carpenter and sailmaker, who was coiling down a line close beside me. Only twenty-two, George was nearer my age than others of the crew, and I already felt I knew him rather well—well enough to ask him a question.

"Our captain," I said. "You come from Shelburne, his home town. What's he like, really?"

George pushed his escaping mop of black hair under the edge of his woollen cap. "Thomas Cunningham? The best man I ever sailed under," he replied, with his easy going smile. He added, "Some say he's too fond of carrying sail in high winds, but I'd trust his judgement in any weather."

I nodded, satisfied.

George went on, more soberly, "But he's not young any more. His wife died last fall, and people say this will be his last trip. He plans to settle ashore near his daughters."

I have since wondered whether things might have turned out differently if our captain had been the bold-spirited man George remembered from earlier voyages.

When I next glanced over the *Vernon's* bulwark

the tide had turned and small eddies were sucking about the wharf-spiles. The ebb was tugging at me, too, for I was eager to be outward bound. When the mate sang out, "Cast off!" I fairly jumped for the nearest hawser. Then, while the *Vernon* slowly sagged away from the wharf, I did my share in setting all plain sail to catch the light and flickering breeze.

In the pull of the tide the brigantine turned her bow this way and that, like a dog eager to pick up a scent and be running free.

"Not that the *Vernon* is any sleek hunting-hound," I admitted silently. "More like Scamp, my fat gunning-dog at home. Not swift, nor beautiful, but faithful and staunch." (Already I had a seaman's pride in his vessel.)

The *Vernon* had been named for her Shelburne builder and owner, Augustus Vernon. She was almost new, having made only one previous trip— as a fishing schooner to the Labrador coast. After that she had been refitted as a brigantine—a two-masted craft, square-rigged on the foremast, schooner-rigged on the mainmast—and chartered for this West Indian voyage. She was not large— scarcely sixty feet long and less than ten feet in the beam. Like most Nova Scotian vessels of her day, she had a square stern, a single deck and she lacked any fancy fittings. She had not been built for looks, but to carry heavy cargoes and to fight her way through stormy seas.

Once the sails were set, we could only wait for the breeze which should come up with the sun. I was still boy enough to enjoy a scramble about masts and rigging. I stepped aft to where the mate stood. "Asking leave to climb to the fore top-gallant crosstree for a look around." I almost added, "John," as I had always addressed this family friend by his first name. But I remembered to say the proper "Mister." Aboard ship not even the captain called the mate by his first name, although sometimes the two were brothers.

John brought his grey eyes down to mine. "Lay aloft, Ben," he gave permission. Then, with a twinkle and half smile, he added, "Keep to the weather-side. If a gust strikes, I don't want you making a hole in that pretty water."

My new seaboots rattled quickly up the foremast shrouds. Once astride the crosstree, I sent my first look toward the harbor mouth where the open sea ran away over the far skyline, and to the shores I was impatient to see. Below me, Mr. MacLeod's "pretty water" looked hard as granite and a long, long way down.

Everything on the *Vernon's* deck appeared flattened and shrunk. In the bow Eddie Norton was busy about the capstan. The sun sparkled on the brown arc of tobacco juice he spat toward the larboard rail. Eddie was a hollow-cheeked man, a bit stooped, a bit bow-legged in his stiff seaboots. He was in his forties and seemed very old to me. Eddie himself had given me no friendly word or look, but now his blue stocking-cap seemed to be nodding up at me in a most amiable way. Where the mainsail's big shadow blackened the after-deck, Mr. MacLeod and George MacKay stood talking.

"I didn't climb up here to get a gull's eye view of my shipmates," I reminded myself. I turned to gaze about the crowded waterfront. To my young country eyes Halifax was a big city, its streets always bright with the garrison's scarlet uniforms, the British navy's blue, and the colorful dress of seamen off foreign merchant ships. On that morning the faint call of a bugle came from the Citadel crowning the city, and I could see a red line of marching soldiers trickled down the slopes of the fortress. The music of fifes and the roll of drums came to me on the sharp air, and I whistled their tune, happy and excited.

Light catspaws of wind ruffled the open harbor, but in the lee of the shore ships floated on their calm reflections, and a tangle of their mirrored masts snaked toward the *Vernon*—masts of schooners, brigs and barques; of great full-rigged ships and neat English packet boats.

From the opposite shore came the Dartmouth ferry—the first steamship I had ever seen—choking and puffing, under the curtain of foul smoke that fell from her stack. The Halifax waterfront was buzzing with talk that Samuel Cunard would soon be starting a steam-packet service to England, but all the seamen I knew scoffed at the new-fangled "tea-kittles." I was ready to scoff too—until a hard fact struck me. "No matter how dirty and ridiculous that ferry looks, *she* is moving, while the *Vernon* has to wait for the wind."

Off the dockyard two of her Majesty's frigates were readying to join the Bermuda squadron. A sudden March gust snatched at my stocking-cap and pierced my thick pea jacket. It made me glad that the *Vernon*, like the naval ships, would be sailing to southern waters. Bermuda, Cienfuegos— these were both names I liked to hear rolling off sailors' tongues.

"When I come home, I'll have ports to name and yarns to tell," I bragged to myself. I pictured the looks my stories would bring to the faces of my family. All at once I had a great desire to see those faces, and they suddenly seemed a long way off.

The mate's voice rose to me, "Lay down from aloft there, Ben." Then, "All hands stand by to square sails." As I slid down the stays, my twinge of homesickness was lost in the excitement of being outward bound at last.

As our sails took the rising breeze, ships and shore began to slip by, and water purled along our hull. The brigantine's new sails were beautiful in the morning sunlight. I said so to Eddie as, side by side, we coiled and belayed lines in the starboard rail.

He cast a sour look at the foremast's surveying squares, and spat a distainful brown stream. "Wait till you're furling them beauties in a gale," he told me darkly. "Fighting and fisting 'em, hanging on by your toenails and eye-winkers, while the *Vernon* drives her yardarms under, trying to wash you off."

I laughed at this dismal picture. "You can't deny we've got a fair wind for our offing," I pointed out.

"Fair, but sharp enough to shave ye!" Eddie growled. Then he added, "There's one thing I *will* admit: if we don't all die of yellow fever where we're going, I'll be *warm* for a spell." He turned away glumly, rolling his stocking cap down and hunching his jacket about his ears. Plainly he didn't put much stock in the opinion of his shipmate, Ben Peach. I soon found that Eddie was one of those men who are never content unless they have something to grumble about.

I was still standing by the lee rail watching the city's outer wharves run past, when someone stepped beside me.

"Your first trip, boy?" our black cook asked, turning his broad back to the wind and smiling down on me. I have never seen a more powerful built man than Jim Tyler. Beside Jim, John MacLeod's six feet and broad shoulders seemed to shrink. Nor have I ever known a kindlier man.

I grinned up at him. "For two years I've been a rockweed sailor." (This is what we called a crewman on our small coastal packets which never ventured far from shore.) "This is my first West Indies cruise."

Jim gazed shoreward. "I remember *my* first trip, thirty-odd years ago. I was a skinny little cabin boy on a barque." He gestured ahead to a break in the Halifax shoreline. "See there, where that ship's boat is loading water casks? *We* took on water there, and I ain't never been so scared before nor since."

I looked up at him. I could see nothing frightening where he had pointed.

"Right there, 'longside Freshwater River, so as to be a warning to mariners, the pirate Jordan had been hanged. When I stepped out of the boat and looked up, there he was—rotting and tattling in his gibbet chains! I yelled and run—and I didn't stop till I was well under the stowed sail in the bow of our shore-boat. The bosun near laughed his head off when he found me there." Jim laughed too at the frightened child he had been.

"A pirate!" I said. "Then he deserved to swing on a gibbet."

"That's right," Jim agreed. "But *I* didn't deserve to see him."

I spoke what came into my careless head.

"Suppose the *Vernon* has a brush with pirates, Jim? Wouldn't that be something to tell the folks when we get back to Halifax?" I smiled up at him, half-joking, half-thinking such an adventure *would* make a great yarn to spin later, like the pirate stories I had drunk in when my father's shipmates gathered about our fireplace on a winter's night.

Jim's face closed and greyed. "Hey," he said sternly, "don't never mention such things. I don't want no truck with pirates." He shivered in the wind, turned away and disappeared down the galley companionway.

"I'd better tighten that slack lip of mine," I scolded myself. "Already it has put me on the wrong side of Eddie Norton and Jim Tyler."

Much of the zest was gone from my morning. Rather sadly I watched Chebucto Head as it dropped astern. That afternoon, when Sambro Light—our last landmark—sank below the sea, I tried to believe it was only the salt wind that brought tears to my eyes.

2
Life at Sea

Next morning not another sail was in sight. The *Vernon* had the wide sea to herself. Her canvas leaned gently against the sky, but now and then her bow thumped down into a sea and her bowsprit dipped to toss sparkling spray across her deck.

"We're spanking away for Cuba, Ben!" George MacKay called to me happily, when he came on watch, his black eyes shining.

As the day wore on, clouds gathered and fitful blasts began to whistle and whine in the rigging. By sunset these blasts were roaring and had forced us to shorten sail. The seas rose with the wind. The *Vernon* climbed watery hills to coast down their slopes and crash at the bottom. Water flew across the deck, sails slatted, spars groaned. Then she climbed once more.

When I came off watch and left the windy deck

for the smoke and smells of the stuffy forecastle, I doubted if I could trust my stomach. It didn't completely betray me, but for most of the night I lay squamishly awake, listening to the quarrelsome combers seethe and growl along the brigantine's labouring hull. Often I was flung against the vessel's side.

Eddie was cold and wet when he came below. He grumbled, "Why was I such a fool as to follow the sea?" Then, pulling off his sodden boots, he added, "If I ever set these cowhides of mine on dry land again, there they'll stay—even if I have to cut wood for a living." He spat his quid into the galley fire, extracted his plug from a dry inside pocket and bit off another comforting chew.

For once I had no cheerful answer to his complaints. I, too, had been considering the benefits of a job on solid land.

However, we had an unusually fine outward passage, and this half-gale on leaving Halifax was the worst weather we met on the whole voyage. By morning my stomach had settled, and I polished my breakfast plate as usual. When I reached deck I found a brilliant sun in the high blue sky and snow-white foam in the *Vernon's* wake.

Nevertheless, I soon learned that leaving the land for a life at sea meant moving into another world—a world of ocean and sky where the *Vernon* was always at the center of the floor of water, and always under the peak of the sky's dome. Such an empty world that birds and fish came to seem like company, and the playing porpoises that raced our cutwater were friends.

On the *Vernon* we were soon comfortable shipmates, but in many forecastles, with strangers crowded together and cut off from the rest of the world, bitter quarrels broke out. Wise masters and mates kept their crews busy and, although the *Vernon* was newly refitted, we did our share of scraping yards and tarring down.

I was in Mr. MacLeod's watch. He slept aft, near the captain's cabin but, as mate, he was in charge of the forward part of the brigantine. So it was that I saw much more of him than of Captain Cunningham. On the Sabbath, when little work was done aboard ship, the mate often joined the crew gathered about the forward coaming. There his strong tenor led us in singing the old hymns we all knew. Eddie had a true tenor voice; the rest of us followed along as best we could, while Jim snapped his fingers and tapped his foot in time as he sang.

Three days out we hit the northern edge of the Gulf Stream. From then on each day grew warmer and we began to doff our heavy clothes. On my fine-weather tricks at the wheel, I drank in the soft sounds of swaying sails and water gurgling along the hull, the tap-tap of reef-points, and the creak of tackle as the breeze canted.

But there were days and nights of squally weather, when we were sent aloft to furl the foremast's upper sails, clambering and swinging about the tops and yards. I noticed that at night, or in heavy squalls, Mr. MacLeod never sent *me* out on the bowsprit to help furl the jib. It was off a bowsprit, the "widow-maker," that my father had been lost.

The hardest work was on the ropes—the braces which haul the yards around, and the halyards which hoist yards and sails. But even when Jim had not been called on deck, his big hands would often appear beside mine, lending the weight and muscle I still lacked.

I hated crawling up the companionway, half-awake, to stand a rainy night watch. But when my trick was over, how satisfying it was to strip off my wet clothes and turn in under my blanket, knowing I had done a man's job. On fine nights— well, I cannot describe the stars' blue flames overhead and their light across the sea's face, while every wavelet sparkled with phosphorescent diamonds. In spite of all that happened later, this first voyage gave me a lasting love for the wind in the rigging and the surge of the sea.

All one day we lay becalmed in the yellow-stained fringe of the Sargasso Sea, where seaweeds lay like reefs around us. Eddie grumbled, "I've knowed vessels that spent *weeks* trapped in these weeds." But our luck held. On the second morning a wind loitered along and, taking every advantage of it, we worked the *Vernon* clear.

"Now, boys," Mr. MacLeod said happily, "we'll pick up the northeast trade winds and run off six to seven knots an hour until we strike West Indie waters." And so we did.

Schools of flying fish leaped out of the bow-wave's curl to skim along for a hundred yards or more, their wings glistening like rainbows. As they slipped back into the sea, another school would break water to fly to windward, ten to twelve feet above the surface. At night I often heard the quivering sound as they skittered upward, and the hissing of their stiff wings as they soared away in the darkness. Many fell to the deck and sometimes, by the light of a hurricane lantern, I gathered a basketful for breakfast. They were the sweetest fish I ever tasted, and Jim fried them to perfection.

"Don't you *never* get filled up, boy?" he'd ask, smiling down at me.

Despite the wonderful sailing weather, the voyage began to grow monotonous. Eddie told me, "Watch for Cap Haytien. That'll likely be our first landfall—and when we strike the Windward Passage, pray for a fresh northerly. A calm in those waters can fry the grease right out of ye."

Our small vessel carried few navigational aids. It was said that captains sailed by "prayer, experience and instinct." Grey-haired Captain Cunningham must have been one of the best at this. Twenty-five days out of Halifax we sighted land—not Cap Haïtien but, better, the northeast coast of Cuba.

This appeared as a long green line with grey-blue hills behind it. We followed it eastward past sandy islands and, all the way, surf made a wide white band along the shores. Captain Cunningham stopped beside me once and explained, "The trade winds that pushed us south blow steadily on this coast of Cuba. They keep the surf forever rolling. That's why Cuba's ports lie on its southern and western parts."

The breeze held fair as we ran down the Windward Passage and rounded the rocky headlands of Cuba's eastern end. Then we set our course westward for Cienfuegos, which lies about two-thirds of the way along the southern coast.

Now, when off watch, we went through our sea chests and sat about the deck mending our clothes and replacing buttons. I felt my mother near as I awkwardly used the needles and threads, the buttons and yarns she had packed in my ditty box. George MacKay, the ends of his black curls bleached in the sun and salt winds, and his nose always peeling from sunburn, often sat beside me in the mainsail's shadow, where we chattered and joked like two boys. But George mostly used his sail-needles, his *palm* and *fid* on the *Vernon's* canvas and rope suit.

I was the only one of the *Vernon's* crew who had

not sailed these waters before. The others must have tired of my questions and exclamations at the beauties of the far mountains with their white cloud-caps, and their green foothills running shoreward. They smiled at the way I gulped down the land breezes, heavy with perfume from unfamiliar blossoms.

Three days after we had set our westward course, Eddie called from the bow, "Cienfuegos fort, bearing west by no'the!"

The end of our outward voyage was in sight, but that day's sun was already plummeting behind the mountains, and complete darkness would soon fall. We stowed our upper sails and jogged offshore, waiting for daylight to reveal the harbor entrance.

3
Cienfuegos

Morning brought a light southerly wind, just what we needed, for Cienfuegos lies at the northern head of a long bay. As we sailed toward the town, the shore was lined by graceful palms that swayed their tall bare trunks and dusted the blue sky with their fronds. The sapphire bay washed creamy sand beaches. At the distant head of the bay, low white houses clustered on the rising land.

"This must be one of the most beautiful spots in the world," I told myself.

However, when we reached "the narrows" the breeze died and the current began to pull dangerously ashore. The mate ordered the boat lowered. Under the glaring sun the crew, in relays, strained at the oars to keep the *Vernon* towed clear. The air grew motionless with heat. When I took my turns at an oar, sweat poured down my bare chest and back, and collected on the thwart under me. The land smells, which had come fresh and fragrant to the *Vernon* offshore, were stiffling now. Everything, near or distant, quivered in the heat haze. Beauty might be all around us still, but I no longer saw it.

We all heartily welcomed the fair breeze that sprang up late that afternoon. We had worked the *Vernon* well up into the bay before we ran out anchor for the night.

Next morning we sailed past the first wharf, where a Spanish brig and a Dutch barque were already berthed and discharging cargoes. We warped the *Vernon* alongside the next wharf and made fast.

Almost at once a burly man stepped aboard. As Captain Cunningham came forward to meet him, the mate said under his breath and to no one in partiucular, "How did Mr. Strachan come to pick *him* as consignee?"

I looked more closely. I judged the heavy, barrel-chested man to be in mid-thirties, about Mr. MacLeod's age. He was dressed in light pants and jacket—common garb in Cuba, I learned, but strange then to my eyes. A rough red beard fell over his upper chest, glinting even in the shadow of his wide sombrero.

"Francisco David, Merchant," he introduced himself, thrusting out a thick brown hand, with a too hearty air of fellowship. Our usually polite captain ignored the hand with a cool nod. I could tell from his face the Cuban felt offended at this, but almost immediately he gave a gusty laugh, showing wide-spaced, stained teeth. Then, feeling my fascinated gaze upon him, he turned swiftly toward me. There was no laughter in his narrow, yellowish eyes, and I was glad to hurry forward to my work. He and the captain then moved about the brigantine, discussing cargo and prices.

When Mr. David left the *Vernon*, my eyes followed him up the wharf. Midway, a man stepped from the shadow of a warehouse and the two stood for some minutes earnestly talking, with now and then a toss of the head toward our vessel. I don't remember just when Mr. David introduced this man to Captain Cunningham, "Senor Augustin Lopez—my first mate, you might say. Not that I ever go to sea!" he hastened to add. "Not me. *I* like to feel solid ground under my boots." He laughed gustily.

Senor Lopez was slightly built, with copper-colored skin, heavy-lidded eyes and thick lips under a dropping mustache. He and Mr. David spent a great deal of time about the Vernon and the wharf as we unloaded. They checked the casks and boxes of dried fish, and the barrels of herring, then saw that their peons stowed them properly in Mr. David's warehouse. Often I found myself watching the two, and listening to them talk, although I understood no Spanish. Lopez glared at me when I came too near and once I heard him repeat angrily something about "el muchacho." (Later, Mr. MacLeod assured me "el muchacho" meant nothing worse than "boy".)

Whenever Mr. David came aboard the *Vernon*, I tried to keep out of his way. So did Eddie. "Reminds me of a *dogfish*," was his poor opinion of the merchant.

Once on night watch something made me say to John MacLeod, "Mister, what do you think of our consignee? I don't like the two-faced way he claps me on the shoulder. Nor his rough laugh. And have you noticed, John—sir—how he looks at our captain when he thinks no one is watching?"

The mate was slow in answering, but his tone was light. "I can't say I like our Mr. David. But, Ben, you don't have to think highly of every man you do business with. You'll probably have to put up with worse than Mr. David before you've made as many West Indian voyages as I have." He added, "At least he can speak English. That makes it eaiser for me than trying to talk my crippled Spanish."

"That's another thing, " I told him. "I hate not being able to understand what he says about me to Mr. Lopez. Even when Mr. David uses English, it has a twist and run to it, different from what I've always heard."

John laughed as he turned away. "There's other English besides the Nova Scotia brand, Ben."

Though I never learned Mr. David's background, I think he must have been one of the many European seamen who, once ashore in Cuba, deserted ship. Mostly these men lived with native women, although a few married into Spanish families.

Finally our unloading was completed. I had thought we would be taking on our return cargo at Cienfuegos, but some disagreement arose between Captain Cunningham and Mr. David. (Decisions about the ship's business while in foreign ports were left to the captains of Nova Scotian craft.) Despite Mr. David's arguments and wheedlings, and his final anger, our captain announced that he would load sugar and rum at Kingston.

The mate seemed pleased at the captain's decision. Later he told me, "I'm glad you'll see Jamaica on this trip, Ben. It's the most beautiful of all the West Indie islands."

"And Mr. David and Senor Lopez won't be there!" I added happily.

On the following morning, as our sails dropped from the yards and caught the breeze, the palm trees were tossing their plumes in the freshening wind. By afternoon we had passed Cienfuegos fort, and were heading for Jamaica, ninety miles away.

4
A Strange Vessel

No day ever dawned in greater beauty, or gave less warning of what it would bring, than did the third day of May. Only Eddie and I—he at the idle wheel and I at the bow watch—were awake. Like the crew, the *Vernon* herself seemed asleep. Cool to my bare feet, the deck was drenched by the dew that falls so heavily in those latitudes. Above me the limp sails, spread to catch any possible wind, hung as wet as if we had just dipped them overboard.

I leaned across a windlass-bitt, looking carelessly toward the pearly horizon. The sea, empty of all ships save the *Vernon*, was a great mirror for the dawn-tinted sky. Jamaica lay below the southern skyline astern. This gem of an island had lived up to John's praise and at Kingston, Captain Cunningham had found a friendly merchant and taken aboard his return lading—eighty puncheons of rum.

We had left harbor with all sails drawing. But here we were, eight days out and, during all that time, not one good wind had helped us on our way. Often we had lain, as we did now, helpless in a flat calm, on a sea that gleamed as if greased. For long hours at a time the crew had sprawled on deck, shifting with the mainsail's shadow. Several days ago, Cape San Antonio had appeared westward, but we wore away its distance slowly. One squally wind following a great cloudburst had set us past the Isla de Piños. That wind had died as suddenly as it had sprung up and left us rolling in a heavy swell with slatting sails and a banging main boom.

Since then we had made little headway, although the Isla de Piños was now lost astern and Cape San Antonio was clearly outlined ahead. With one good wind we could work around Cuba's western end and be homeward bound.

Some seamen claim they have called up a fair wind by whistling from the topmast, by driving a knife into the mainmast, or by tossing a coin overboard. I was tempted to try one—or all—of these devices, but Eddie had warned me, "I've knowed every one of them charms to rouse great gales—even hurricanes in these southern waters."

The sun came up out of the sea, dripping blood red over the silvery ocean. I noticed that a current was drawing us nearer the Cuban shore with its dangerous reefs and islands. I looked up at the slack sails and made a seaman's prayer. "Put a wind where it belongs, Lord," I pleaded. As if in answer, a sail slapped against the mast, but when I looked up hopefully, I found this was only because *Vernon* had yawed slightly to the current's pull.

The brigantine came awake. Jim began rattling pans in the galley and good smells wafted up the hatchway. The mate came on deck and laughed at something Eddie said. George's black head appeared above the forecastle coaming.

The Carribean sun comes up with a splendid burst of color, but it pales swiftly. The ocean tints faded, the shore to starboard took on sharp outlines while the trees that had earlier seemed black turned green.

I decided we were off a deserted shore. No life stirred anywhere. I looked again. There at the tip of the nearest island—was that speck a rock my eyes hadn't caught before? Or was it a boat that hadn't been there for them to catch? Was that flash from the sun—or a wet oar blade? The distance was too great for me to be sure. Whatever it had been, it had disappeared behind the island, or blended into the shoreline.

Eddie went below for breakfast. Jim's curly head and shining face, with its broad smile, rose from the forecastle steps. "Morning boy," he said, nodding as he met my eye. Then appeared the usual platter with its mug and coffee pot. Jim shuffled aft with Captain Cunningham's early cup of coffee. "I like to take good care of my captain, when they's taking good care of me," Jim explained, as he did each morning.

When I looked again there was no doubt as to whether what I had seen was a rock or a boat. What now looked like a small bug with three long legs on each side, was crawling away from the shore—a boat with six long sweeps out.

I had thought that any craft, any sign of life, would be a welcome sight. But what was this stranger creeping slowly closer over a silken water? A chill struck across the warming deck. I glanced swiftly up at our topsails, hoping they might be rounding to the upper air. The dew was drying from the canvas, but every inch of it still hung slack.

At that moment the mate hailed me from the stern, "Below with you, Ben. Get some of Jim's flapjacks before Eddie polishes them all off."

This almost made me forget my uneasiness, but with one foot on the companionway I stopped.

"A boat, Mr. MacLeod."

"Where away?" He walked forward.

"Well off the starboard quarter," I pointed.

Just as mine had done, his eyes went from the distant boat to the lifeless upper sails. "Nip aft, Ben. Tell the captain there's a stranger approaching." As I moved to obey, his voice came back to me in the oddly muffled echo thrown off by wet sails—almost a ghostly whisper. "Ask him for his spyglass."

Mr. MacLeod held the captain's glass to his eye for a long minute, while his body stiffened. He said only, "Lay below now, Ben. Get some breakfast into you. But this morning I want no lallygagging to tease the cook."

"Aye, sir."

There was no need to tell me against wasting time below deck.

"Boy," Jim told me, "them's *big* flapjacks. They wasn't meant to go down like that."

I continued to gobble pancakes—and without praising them, although I knew how much Jim liked his cooking to be appreciated. Many a time since I've wished I could taste Jim's flapjacks once more, but that morning I wanted only to fill the empty space the night had left in my stomach, and be back on deck.

When I told Eddie I had sighted a boat, he gulped the last of his tea and hurried up the ladder. I was close on his heels as he walked aft.

George was at the wheel. In the stern Captain Cunningham was smoking his after-breakfast pipe. The mate stood silently beside him. All eyes were fastened on the coming boat. I was amazed to see how it had gained on us during my brief time below.

The captain was thin-lipped as he turned to answer a remark from George. "It's true the Cape San Antonio area was known as a hive of pirates, but a few years ago the Spanish admiral claimed he had smoked them all out. The British West Indies fleet has a number of ships always cruising these waters. It is most unlikely...." But Captain

Cunningham sounded uncertain. He knocked out his pipe and pocketed it.

"Pirates." The word weighing on our minds had been said, and it clanged in my ears.

The mate straightened and raised the spyglass. "A yawl," he told us. "No doubt it has a lugsail and a mast stick stowed for'ard, but the crew are using sweeps." As if talking to himself he added, "In a calm, sweeps can always overtake sailing craft."

Unbidden the picture of the Dartmouth ferry came to my mind, and I wished for her engine.

Eddie said quietly, "I've always heard the West Indies pirates lurk behind islands and capes, ready to pounce out." Now that there was really something to worry about, Eddie had stopped grumbling.

The mate lowered the glass. "Captain," he said, "have we *any* firearms aboard? A fowling piece or two in your cabin?"

Regretfully, Captain Cunningham spread empty hands. "Not even a pistol, or a dress-sword, though I have both at home. Who could have foreseen any need for arms aboard the *Vernon*?"

"So we're sitting ducks," the mate muttered.

The boat had come to within hailing distance. The first shout from her was unintelligible. Captain Cunningham cupped his ear with his hand. The thickset man in the yawl's stern rose to his feet, made a trumpet of his hands and yelled again.

"Revenue?" the captain looked puzzled but relieved, and I almost laughed as the hard knot in my stomach loosened.

The man in the yawl waved an arm and called what sounded like orders. I caught words, "revenue cutter" and "papers."

Captain Cunningham shrugged. "I never thought I'd be taken for a smuggler! But I'm sure my clearance papers from both Cienfuegos and Kingston are in order."

He turned as if to go to the cabin for the papers. But at that instant I saw something—something that made me forget that a crew member doesn't grab his captain by the arm.

Before I could bring any words to my lips, the mate said sharply, "Revenue cutter be damned! On this foresaken shore ... seven men in a boat that small." He drew in his breath as if in sudden need of air. "And all armed to the teeth!"

I closed my mouth, which had been hanging

open like a fish's. "Captain," I said, letting go his arm now that I had his attention, "that man in the yawl's stern—as he turned and the sun struck his beard—didn't you see, sir? That's Mr. David! Mr. David who said he *never* went to sea."

Again the mate swung the spyglass to his eye. "Ben's right, Cap'n. And that's the precious Lopez at the bow sweep."

By now none of us needed a spyglass, so rapidly were the rowers closing on the *Vernon*. Captain and mate stared into each other's eyes for a long second with hard fixed stares—not desperate, but sober indeed.

Then Mr. MacLeod said quietly, "George and Eddie, break out the kedge-anchor."

He turned to the captain. "If we heave it down into the yawl we might stave and sink her. Or the flukes might disable a man or two and lessen the odds against us. At the very least it should keep her crew busy while we find something else to offer them."

Turning to the cook, who had joined us on the deck, he asked, "Any pots of hot water, Jim? No coals? Your meat cleavers and knives then."

Then, to me, he said, "Fetch us belaying pins."

"Mr. MacLeod," the captain broke in sadly, "if these are pirates, any struggle against them means certain death for us all." I thought his glance rested on me as if I was especially in his mind. He continued, "If we offer no resistance, the robbers may be satisfied with the vessel and cargo. They may let us have the *Vernon's* small-boat. Or they might set us ashore."

"Cap'n," the mate pleaded, "our only chance...."

But we were to have *no* chance. A sharp cry from Eddie and a hard downward swing of his arm sent us all sprawling to the deck. Bullets swept that part of the *Vernon* where we had been standing, foolishly exposed. "So they have muskets as well as small arms," I thought. We could only cower behind masts and housing, certain that the shouted "revenue" and "papers" had been a trick to gain time and draw nearer. Even if the mate had had our kedge-anchor to hand, he could not have thrown it over the hail of bullets.

5
Plundered

The lack of return fire must have assured the pirates that the brigantine was helpless. With the crew whooping and yelling like wild men, the yawl pulled boldly alongside, and Mr. David scrambled over our midship rail.

He was no oily merchant now, but an arrogant ruffian dressed as such. Instead of the wide sombrero he had always worn in Cienfuegos (which would be worse than useless in a sea-wind) a vivid red cap now closely covered his head. His open shirt showed a bullneck, great muscled shoulders and a mat of coarse red chest-hair that met the long tangled beard.

We had got to our feet, angry but helpless. David looked us all over, planted his boots wide apart and raised a silver-handled pistol from his belt. Then he laughed a gust of hateful, gloating satisfaction. Frightened though I was, that laugh made me ache to shut it off by choking him.

Two of his men took their places on either side of him. Each had a pistol in hand, ugly knives and dirks thrust into his belt, and a cutlass at his side. I saw that all the pirates wore similar arms. All were clad in open shirts and short breeches, rancid with sweat and dirt, and—except for David—had knotted handkerchiefs about their heads.

They looked the cutthroats they were, yet nothing about their harsh face was as merciless as the half-smile, half-snarl on their leader's lips, as he stood and glared at Captain Cunningham.

"So you are a revenue agent now, Mr. David?" our captain said. He looked suddenly older, but his voice was strong, and it carried such scorn that the pirate leader shifted his feet.

"Yes. This is how I get my revenue." He laughed as if he had made a great joke. He went on, "I am now Captain Francis Dennis. *Don't forget that.*" He rubbed his cutlass-hilt threateningly. "The merchant Francisco David belongs in Cienfuegos. He is often called away, up or down the coast, on business—revenue business! Few people suspect that he has any connection with Captain Dennis, the pirate."

He gestured toward where the yawl lay, out of sight under the *Vernon's* quarter. "You remember Señor Lopez, my mate? He'll be aboard in good time."

Then his face darkened. He said harshly to the captain, "So you thought to give us the slip, sailing off to Jamaica with my money. But it didn't work out, did it? Any vessel is welcome so near our headquarters." He waved his pistol toward an island a few miles ahead. "It saves us trouble. When I recognized the *Vernon*, I knew you had not escaped me after all!" He made it sound as if Captain Cunningham had suspected his plans and had tried to thwart them—even as if the captain had wronged him.

Motioning impatiently to show that he had no more time to spend in talk, Dennis said, "Now, old man, take me to your cabin. It will be better for you and your crew if you did not spend the many of my doubloons and pieces of eight in Kingston." He laughed his horrible gusty laugh again, and looked around at his men. They joined in his taunting glee, as if they had been awaiting his permission to do so. Indeed, it was already plain that Dennis' men feared him; that he was the strong leader of heartless rogues who lacked the brains to plan or carry out any undertaking of their own.

Each of the band knew a few English words, but only Dennis spoke the language well. It was not until much later, when I read printed accounts, that I learned anything about the origins of the band's members. That morning I knew only that, despite the pirate yarns I had heard, I never could have imagined such evil creatures as these. The mate muttered, "David must have raked the very cinders of hell for his crew."

We had known the sullen Augustin Lopez in Cienfuegos. With him in the yawl was powerful but simple-minded Pablo, whose other name I never learned because—but that came later.

Juan Arman was swarthy, with lank black hair and a greasy, thin-bearded face. He was called simply Juan to distinguish him from truculent Juan Romero, with the great silver loops in his ears, who came from the Canary Isles.

Francisco Daores, middle-sized and square-built, had thick lips, hooded eyes and a face dark-stained with passion. I never learned what his background might have been before he cast his lot with Dennis.

Lorenzo Fernandes came from Cuba's neighboring island, Puerto Rico. He was small and looked older than the others, but was quick as a cat about the deck of a vessel.

As I have said, I learned these facts only later. That morning the freebooters all looked alike to me, since cruelty and wickedness had stamped each of them.

With his pistol at Captain Cunningham's back, Dennis ordered Juan Romero and Daores to allow them below. Fernandes and Juan Arman were stationed amidships where we five huddled, helpless. The brigantine lay motionless. Like her crew, she seemed caught in some evil enchantment.

John MacLeod broke the spell. "Men!" Because of the watching pirates, he scarcely moved his lips, but he caught our full attention. "We'll rush the two amidships. That will give us four pistols and four cutlasses before the two men from the yawl can climb over the side. Or the three from the cabin reach the deck."

Jim's smile flashed and his shoulders hunched. My heart pounded as I crouched a bit and dug my toes against the deck for a quick spring. We were empty-handed and the pirates heavily armed, but Jim and the mate were unusually powerful men, and I was sure each of the *Vernon's* crew could give a good account of himself in a fight. Anything was better than standing like helpless sheep.

Beside me George had gathered himself as I had done, but suddenly he went limp. "Mister," he said (like the mate, barely moving his lips) "the captain. Three to one in the cabin ... the first sound of a scuffle...."

The mate's squared jaw went slack. Jim's chest collapsed like a spilled sail, and his big black hands fell in a hopeless gesture. At that instant the captain appeared from the cabin. Dennis, pistol still in hand, was close behind him. Our only possible chance to regain the *Vernon* was gone.

We were herded into the bow and tied. The yawl was worked back and made fast to the brigantine's stern. Lopez and clumsy Pablo climbed aboard and joined their comrades on the deck of the captured vessel.

The pirates then began a crazy plundering. They yelled in wild Spanish, or laughed and whooped; they ran and danced and jumped about the deck, slashing aimlessly with whirling cutlasses. Yet, in spite of the confusion, they thoroughly ransacked the *Vernon*, from the after-cabin to the forecastle peak. They gathered the captain's clothes, his instruments and gold watch. They stripped the forecastle berths, and found the few little treasures that the crew kept in their sea chests.

They dumped their loot in a heap upon the foredeck, to be divided. There was little of real value. I noted that the leather bag of coins, which Dennis had in one one hand when he came from the after-cabin, was not put upon the pile, and that the captain's watch soon disappeared. I suspected that Dennis' riffraff were easily deceived, or fobbed off, and got precious little booty. The hot black eyes and greedy lips of Daores as he pawed Captain Cunningham's shore-going suit suggested that one of the band knew how to get his share.

As if to forestall any discontent with the scanty plunder, Dennis shouted, "And don't forget, my hearties, there are eighty puncheons of rum in the hold!" He added something in Spanish, perhaps making sure that all his men understood the promise of more loot.

6
The Pirate's Anchorage

The pirates had hardly finished dividing their booty when a light breeze sprang up. (I thought bitterly that this would have saved the *Vernon*, but had been denied us, only to come to the aid of our enemies). The sails stirred, then rounded. The brigantine shook herself and came to life. We were untied and, under Dennis' blasphemous orders, John MacLeod was put at the wheel while the rest of us worked the *Vernon*, with the yawl in tow. Captain Cunningham was treated as one of the crew—except that Dennis cursed him most savagely of all. Not one of the raiders so much as lifted a finger to help. They all lolled about the deck, aiming a blow or kick at us as we passed.

The wind soon dropped and we lay once more becalmed. The sun went down behind Cape San Antonio, now only a few miles ahead. I wondered sadly, "Was it only this morning that I stood on the *Vernon's* bow and plotted our course in my mind; past Cape San Antonio and Havana, through the Florida Straits to the Gulf Stream, and home?" From Dennis' comments I knew the pirate hideaway was near. "We'll never tack the *Vernon* around San Antonio," I told myself with heavy certainty.

Dennis sent Jim below to cook a meal, while Juan Romero of the silver earrings sat on the companionway, pistol across knee. We were given a little food, then, as darkness deepened, we were chained to the deck and two men were set to guard us.

Dennis warned, "No gabbing. My men will skewer any talkers to the deck."

I suppose he feared that among us we might hatch some scheme for escape. It was true that many hot fantasies of overcoming or outwitting our captors marched through my mind. I had heard tales of how men had escaped from desperate situations—but only because their captors had been careless or drunk. Dennis was ruling his men with an iron hand, and he himself doled out their rations of rum—from one of the *Vernon's* casks. In turn, each of my hazy plots had to be abandoned. Despair settled on me, blacker than the night.

At last I fell asleep, to dream that my mother and sisters were in danger and I, bound to my garret bed, was powerless to save them. I awakened, sweating and thrashing against my chains, dry-mouthed and wet-eyed. Dawn tinged the sky pink.

The day, empty of hope, started like the one before. First a morning of stark calm, then a light, variable breeze. For the *Vernon's* crew there was endless bracing of yards and jibing of mainsail— to catch every air. From the outlaws, scowls and sneers, blows and Spanish oaths. For me, there was stifled anger and—like something eating away inside me with sharp, never-resting teeth—fear of the pirates' pistols and cutlasses.

During the afternoon we drew abreast of an island, scarcely a mile from the Cuban mainland. With Dennis beside John MacLeod at the wheel, we worked the *Vernon* around a point of the island, through a long, winding channel and into the mouth of a horseshoe anchorage.

In other circumstances I would have thought the spot beautiful, for wooded headlands bracketed a white beach where palms waved gently, their green-feather tops brushing the sky. The anchorage was plainly an ideal retreat for sea-robbers. Passing ships would never suspect that the island hid such a haven, while the masts and spars of a captured vessel would blend with the palm trunks and branches.

When the wind died completely, Dennis ordered us to launch the small boat. As this splashed down into the water, a great flock of wading birds rose from the nearest shore and vanished over the trees. They seemed to mourn for us with their eerie, wavering cries.

Daores was put in command of the boat and we were told to tow the brigantine into the head of the cove. When I took my oar every muscle in my body was already aching from the incessant work at the yards; my head was pounding from lack of sleep—and from Lopez's well-aimed blows. The sun beat fiercely down on us and was as fiercely reflected from the glassy water. Over the boat's side, where my dipping oar formed small whirlpools, the sea was crystal green above the sandy bottom. It was all I could do to keep from dropping my oar and plunging downward. I knew the scowling Daores would shoot me the instant I moved. But to rest on the white sand, under the cool green water....

"Ben!" Mr. MacLeod's voice came to me across his shoulder from the thwart before my blurring eyes. The word was scarcely audible but it carried authority. I came out of my dream—and was ashamed. I had been doing little more than lifting my oar and letting it drop. To keep Daores from noticing this, Captain Cunningham was straining to redouble his efforts, though he was near exhaustion. In one short word—my name—the mate had reminded me that we must each bear our share of the misery that had befallen us. The failure of one would bring our captor's anger upon all of us.

I put my weary back and arms into my rowing, taking my stroke from John's.

We towed the Vernon to within thirty feet of the shore. Here her bow took the sand, and we kedged her in until only her stern was afloat. ("What is running through the mate's mind," I wondered, "as he handles the kedge-anchor which he wanted to use as a weapon against the pirates?")

The *Vernon* had stranded on an even keel but we

shored her at the bows. We had no trouble finding props for this. Timbers strewed the shore, and lighter pieces of lumber had been tossed into rough piles along the beach. Charred and broken ships' ribs protruded from the sand. Just above tide line the smashed strakes of a longboat lay in a rotting tangle of canvas and cordage. Plainly this buccaneers' lair had been used for a long time, and had been the last anchorage for many crafts.

In an opening among the trees, a large goods-yard had been cleared. This held heaps of ships' gear, sails and ropes, as well as tiers of casks. "Cargoes of several vessels," I thought, "probably awaiting reshipment."

As night fell we were again given food, then chained to the deck. Only Juan Romero and Daores were left aboard to guard us. The other pirates swung over the side and splashed ashore. Soon I saw firelight flickering through the palms. I wished briefly I could be beside it, for the night air had cooled. But I was too weary to really care. I hugged my ragged jersey about me and fell headlong into sleep.

I awakened to another day of dread and toil. We were ordered to strip the *Vernon* of sails and rigging, then to fix the boom-tackles in preparation for discharging cargo. Jim and Eddie were sent down into the hold to load the sling while John and I, at the windlass, hoisted the heavy puncheons above deck. Captain Cunningham was given the hardest task, for he must swing the boom out over the rail. The puncheons were then lowered to George on the beach alongside. (It sticks in my mind that Dennis must have had some of his band working ashore, or the puncheons could not have been so quickly rolled into the yard.)

In the steaming heat the work was cruel. Before long we were all moving in a sort of stupor. More than once my arms refused to work faster and I caught the flat of Lopez's hand across my ear and felt my head spin. But our captain fared worst of all. Dennis clearly bore him a special spite— perhaps the pirate leader recognised that the gentlemanly shipmaster was still the better man, despite his failing strength. Swinging the boom sling with its load, first clear of the hold, then across the deck and out over the rail, was almost beyond the strength of one man. Yet if Captain Cunningham faltered, the black-humored Dennis was beside him with a blow for malingering and a horrible ranting of Spanish and English curses.

More than once I heard John grind his teeth and swallow his rage with a gulp. My own heart felt near to bursting for our kind captain. But none of us dared try to ease his load for fear the angry pirates would kill him—and us.

There was nothing to mark one of the next three days from another. Under the pirates' blows and mockery, we worked until we were ready to drop. Then, late in our fourth afternoon in the anchorage, the last puncheon was rolled up the beach. The *Vernon* had been stripped to bare poles, her stores rowed ashore and piled in the yard. Now we were told to toss the galley-gear into the center of a topsail and to bundle it overside to be taken ashore. When this was done we dropped, one by one, over the rail to the beach.

Before leaving, I took one last look down the open hatchway of the empty forecastle. Here I had yarned and sung with my shipmates; here I had often pestered Jim until he snatched up a knife or cleaver in mock anger and chased me up on deck. I looked along the desolate deck, once well-scrubbed and shipshape, now filthy and littered. The *Vernon* seemed to upbraid me for abandoning her—as if I would leave by choice!

Juan's angry, *"Prise! Prise!"* (which I had learned

meant "Quickly!") and the sting of a rope end across my shoulders, sent me down a dangling halyard to the sand under the *Vernon's* side.

I had not set foot on land since the day we kedged the *Vernon* in, and my feet felt grateful for the feel of the earth, as we were herded up the beach to the goods-yard.

I saw that the back end of the yard was not lined by open palms, as were its sides, but by a close-woven green wall of thorn bushes and vines. The *Vernon's* rum puncheons lay along one side. Her sails and rigging had been tossed into untidy heaps. Litter from other ships was strewn about: ropes and blocks, a ship's wheel, broken oars, rudders and pintles. Creeping vines from the jungle wall were claiming shattered casks and a capstan with crumpled pawls.

Blackened sand and sticks marked the site of the nightly fires I had glimpsed. Near the ashes, flies swarmed over moulding food and unwashed pots. At one side was a pile of our clothes and blankets, dirty and torn.

The disgusting picture comes back vividly to me now, but at the time I scarcely saw it. I knew the pirates no longer needed our work, and I stood in sick fear of their next move.

Dennis beckoned to Lopez, and the two walked to the wall of trees. They stood for some minutes, out of earshot, gesturing and talking, without betraying anything of the mischief they were surely hatching. Finally Lopez's surly face lighted in a smile of agreement, and he darted a glance of triumph toward the prisoners. Then the two villains returned to where we stood, closely watched by their comrades.

As Dennis gave his next orders, his yellow eyes ran gloatingly over us while his hands hovered near the cocked pistol in his belt. He may have feared that, now we were on land, we would make a desperate attempt for freedom. (Perhaps he wished we would, so he could shoot us down, but our bodies and spirits alike were cowed by the days of brutal labour and cruel blows.)

"You," Dennis pointed a stained finger at George MacKay, "and you, mister mate—over there." He tossed his red-capped head toward the back of the yard and swung his arm. "Coil that cordage. Rope those sails into bundles." He laughed at the two men as they moved to obey. "Do you think you might break through those trees and bushes? You might. Let me tell you there's nothing behind them but jungle and swamp." With a wave in the opposite direction, he added, "Beyond the anchorage there is nothing, even for the best of swimmers, but sharks." He grinned, showing the gap between his discolored teeth.

"Shark yourself," I said under my breath.

Dennis went on, "Daores and Pablo will keep an eye on you both. As for you, mister mate, Daores tells me he would be happy to slit your gullet any time I give him leave." He made the ugly movement of a knife across the throat.

John stared back at him, his grey eyes hard and unflinching as the winter sea.

Dennis' manner then changed to the oiliness I hated above all else about him. "I'm taking the rest of my men, and your shipmates with me in the yawl. We'll gather some ballast in the next cove."

"Ballast?" I said, surprised into speech. "For the *Vernon*?" Might we sail out of the anchorage after all?

"Ben." Captain Cunningham's quiet warning was lost in an angry roar from Dennis, and I bit my lip.

"Or we might look for that anchor we slipped last trip, eh Lopez?" Dennis laughed his odious laugh, at some joke we could not share. He waved his pistol. "The rest of you, get back down the beach, to launch the yawl."

Following Captain Cunningham, and with five pirates close behind us, Eddie, Jim and I made our way to where the buccaneers' craft lay afloat at tide's edge.

7
Murder

If my heart had been leaden before, how can I describe my feelings as we launched the yawl? I had the terrible certainty that we were being got out of the way while savage Daores and willing Pablo killed John and George—probably because they were the two strong and brave enough to head an escape.

I was put at the bow sweep, with Eddie in front of me. (His back had grown pitifully thin, but his only complaint was that the robbers had taken his chewing tobacco.) Beyond Eddie was Jim's ebony shoulder. Against the blistering sun I wore what rags were left of my shirt, but Jim loved the heat and always went stripped to the waist. Captain Cunningham was given the aftersweep, within reach of the taunting tongue and booted foot of Dennis in the stern sheets.

The pirates crouched between the thwarts. None of them rowed, though the yawl moved sluggishly, being water-logged and fouled with weeds. They were all armed, since they were never without weapons and seemed to take pride in the number of cutlasses and knives they could sling about their bodies. Fernandes, the little Puerto Rican, had his pistol loosened in his belt and had laid his cutlass by his hand. Lopez bent forward, elbow on knee, chin on clenched fist and, whenever I looked at him, glowered at me from under his drooping lids.

At Dennis' "Steady as ye go," we settled down to hard rowing.

I tried to catch a last glimpse of the two friends left behind. I was sure that I would never again yarn with George in the mainsail's shadow, never again hear John's, "Well done, Ben. We'll make a seaman of you yet." I thought of John's wife and children, going about their everyday lives in Liverpool. Perhaps even now Mrs. MacLeod was having a cup of tea in our kitchen, for she and mother liked to visit back and forth. I told myself I would give my own life to save the two shipmates left at the pirates' mercy. That was the hardest thing to bear—that each of us was powerless to aid the other.

On the shore the *Vernon* was a naked hull, leaning shoreward, unresponsive to the easy swells that ran in with the tide to lap her hull. "You always carried sail like a lady," I told her in silent tribute.

Dennis snapped me out of my sad thoughts with, "Hard t' starb'd." We swung westward from the anchorage, keeping close to land. After rounding a rocky stretch of shore, we pulled into a wide-mouthed cove where fishing birds were squalling overhead. Though we were less than a mile from the pirate resort, the land here was completely different. Palm fringed sand had been replaced by a swampy shore. Wisps of steam rose above the swamp, although the afternoon heat was lessening as the sun lowered. A drifting mat of leaves marked the entrance to a small creak running inland.

"Ballast!" I thought scornfully. "Where in the world could you find a less likely place for ballast?" I was surer than ever that this trip had been a ruse to break up the *Vernon's* crew, to get most of us out of the way while some brutal scheme was carried out.

Moving the weedy-bottomed yawl was backbreaking work. When Dennis said, "'Vast rowing!" and then, "Ship oars," we gladly obeyed. I pulled my sweep across the boat and leaned forward to rest my arms upon it. There was a second of silence, holding only the drip from oar-blades and the breathing of tired rowers.

Alertness could not have saved us, but we were caught completely off guard. The command to ship oars had been an arranged signal. Dennis sprang to his feet. His cutlass flashed across Captain Cunningham's throat. At the same time Lopez and Juan seized the captain from behind, but there was no need to hold him. The three murderers tossed his limp body overboard in one careless swing.

They turned swiftly on Jim. Fernandes and Juan Romero had grabbed Eddie.

It all happened so suddenly and I was so stunned, that before I could lift my arms from the oar, Eddie lay crumpled on the bottom planks, and Jim was already wounded. The big black man did not die without fighting, and I owe my life to his strength and great heart. He flung his attackers off. The hulking Dennis went reeling back into the stern. The other two floundered between the thwarts. Fernandes and Juan Romero left Eddie's fallen body and leapt to close in on Jim. As he turned to face their knives, the knotted muscles of his great shoulders and biceps gleamed in the sun. But I saw the welling blood from his wounds — and I knew....

Sick horror had bound me to the thwart. Suddenly I realized that these butchers would turn on me next. I sprang to my feet, crazed with terror. Jim turned his head toward me—toward the boy who was his friend. His eyes sought mine in a desperate pleading.

"Oh Jim," I answered him silently, for my throat was swollen shut with grief and fear, "I would help you if I could. Don't you know?"

With a great effort of will, Jim straightened. Again he was able to throw off his attackers, since their numbers and lack of foot-room hampered them. He sent me another pleading look, then he raised his arm and flung himself over the yawl's side.

At the sound of that mighty splash, Jim's message reached my frozen brain. He had been pleading with me to save myself. I sprang for the bow. Juan Romero and Fernandes turned murderous faces toward me, but Jim's leap had set the yawl rocking, and thrown them off balance. Before their evil hands could grasp me, I was on the bow-gunwale. Every ounce of fear-whipped muscle was behind my dive. I had no plan of escape. If I had a thought at all, it was that I would rather drown than be stabbed to death.

I was one of the best swimmers among the boys who played about the Liverpool wharves in summer, and this stood me in good stead. I put considerable distance between me and the yawl before my bursting lungs drove me up for air. The murder boat was still terrifyingly close. I heard shots and saw that the pirates were emptying their pistols into Jim's floundering body. I allowed myself no more than one swift glance and one great gulp of air before I went under again. Now the desire to live and escape was strong in me. Jim had won a chance for me, had given me precious minutes by his brave fight. The water was warm, and although my ragged breeches somewhat hampered my legs, I knew I could keep swimming for hours if need be.

When I next broke water and looked for the

yawl, two of her crew were straightening up after heaving something overboard. "Eddie's gone," I thought numbly. There was no sign of Jim. A yell sounded from the yawl and a bullet whizzed past my forehead sending up a spurt of foam only a few inches beyond. Having killed my three companions, the cutthroats were turning all their attention to me.

I went under before quite filling my lungs and soon had to surface again. Another bullet hit close beside me. Against the shadow of the dark trees, I saw the pale flame as a pistol was fired. I thought, "My head will be a target whenever I surface, and my wake will betray my position."

I had been swimming straight toward shore but, once the yawl's sweeps were manned, I would be overtaken before I could gain land—or I would be within pistol shot as I struggled through the shallows. I had glimpsed, off on one side, a large rock or group of rocks, a few yards in circumference, with ragged tops barely above water. Around this, collected and carried by a tidal eddy, floated a mat of dead swamp grasses, reeds and twigs. This time when I submerged, I turned at a sharp angle and swam with all my might. Among the floating tangle lay my only hope of eluding the men who wanted my life. My lungs were burning, my arms and legs like lead, by the time I had gained the fringe of the flotage. Only then did I dare come up for breath.

By now the sun was gone and night was creeping out from the land. Probably I owed as much to the failing light and the shore's dark shadows as to my manoeuvres. From the yawl my head must have blended with the rock and the shore behind it. The boat passed my hiding place, still heading shoreward.

Juan Romero, in the bow, was peering into the water on either side. Dennis stood in the stern, silhouetted against the red sky, pistol in hand. I thought bitterly, "How he would delight in emptying his pistol into me—to watch me flounder and sink as Jim did!" In the distance and dim light he was little more than a silhouette, but I pictured his shirt and matted chest as I had last seen them, stained with Captain Cunningham's blood. Anger against this man rose in me, sharp and sour as the salt water I had swallowed, and this roused my failing strength.

The fact that the yawl followed my former direction no doubt saved me. The pirates lost considerable time before they decided I was not ahead of them, and turned their boat about. The rock with its encircling driftage then attracted their notice. They began to row toward me, with Dennis shouting violent and profane commands. But I had got some breath back, and my heavy limbs would move again. I went under and made sure that the rock was between me and the yawl before I surfaced. I knew the long sweeps would need a much wider circle in order to round the rock.

Although I could plainly see the yawl and its men when they moved against the sky's afterglow, the rock and I were in the shore's shadows. I blessed the sudden tropical night—at home the lingering May twilight would have revealed my every movement through the glassy water.

Twice I noiselessly circled the rock ahead of the yawl. Movement would not betray me now, for any ripples caused by my swimming could as well have been set up by the sweeps, or by backwash from the rock. But I was growing too weary to continue this horrible game. My heart was pounding hard, though as much from terror as from exertion. I knew that if I reached the point where I must thrash to keep afloat, or gasp for air as I surfaced, I would be finished.

At one place a curve in the rock formed a miniature cove, scarcely the width of my body. A thick mat of sodden grass and reeds floated in this small semi-circle. My instinct was to keep moving ahead of the yawl and out of its reach, but when I next came opposite this curve, I turned, dove, and came up through the reeds. I had hoped there might be a ledge of underwater rock to cling to, or use as a footrest, but deep water came right to the rock face. I turned upon my back and kept only my nose and mouth above the wet debris. I tried not to breathe too quickly or deeply, for in the still air the sound of my laboring breath must surely carry to my pursuers.

When the yawl drew abreast of me I had great difficulty in stealing myself against movement, for it was circling closer than before. So close the sweeps might strike me as they dipped. (I could understand why hunted animals often break and run, when they would be safe if they stayed hidden.)

Then I heard something that gave me hope. "He's drowned," Dennis said, tired of the search. "One of our shots found its mark, or a shark has him." Although he believed me dead, he cursed me viciously—and if ever a voice held baffled murder, I heard it there in the quiet cove.

One of the men made a suggestion in Spanish, and Dennis grunted assent. A pirate on either side of the boat drew his cutlass and, as the yawl once more began to circle the rock, they stabbed downward at random. The swishing blades made long lines and small whirlpools where they probed the water. I could distinguish no figure but that of Dennis in the stern, so I never knew which of these merciless men rowed, and which stabbed the water in hopes of finding the heart of a frightened boy.

They came around to where I lay, rigid with fright and scarcely breathing. The passing thrust of a cutlass came within a foot of my body. It was all I could do not to turn over and thrash away from it, or to cry out. In fact, my shattered nerves would soon have betrayed me.

Dennis gave a muttered order. Apparently it was to abandon the hunt, for the men at the gunwales put their cutlasses away and sat down. The yawl slowly pulled toward the cove's mouth and disappeared into the dusk. The sound of oars, dipping and thudding against the tholepins, faded. The silence was a pain in my ears.

8
The Swamp

Never before or since have I known loneliness to match that which gripped me as the yawl disappeared. God knows I never wanted to see it again, but it left the cove so utterly empty, the sky so unbroken and indifferent.

I no longer had the support of comrades sharing my peril. Remembering the murders I had witnessed, I shook until my teeth chattered. "And the guards have killed John and George," I heard myself say. I was indeed alone. I recalled my mother's teachings and tried to share her faith in God's care, but even he seemed far away from the darkening cove, somewhere beyond the remote sky.

I suspected Dennis's orders to give up the search might have been meant for my ears, to deceive me into betraying myself once I believed danger past.

I made no move until long after the yawl disappeared. I strained my ears with listening, knowing that even the dip of a sweep would come to me across the silent water. The soft lap of the tide was the only sound. After a time, I cautiously circled the rock, pausing often to listen. Satisfied that the murderers had indeed left, I began to swim for shore.

The nearest point lay no more than twenty yards away, but my strength barely brought me there. I crawled out where a thin, ill-smelling trickle oozed from the swamp. There I fell flat, panting and retching up salt water, while trees and cove and starry sky whirled and spun about me.

I soon began to shiver in my wet rags as the night air cooled. As my senses returned, terror caught me again. Even if the pirates *had* returned to their rendevous, they were only around the point. With daylight they would come again in search of me. While night hid me I must get as far as possible from them. But where could I go? Nothing but swamp lay in every direction but seaward—and no hope lay there.

I told myself that the swamp and its water holes could not be any more treacherous than the pirates.

Poisonous snakes and wild animals could not be any crueller. I decided that no matter how uninviting it was, the swamp would be a good thing to have between me and my enemies.

I stumbled to my feet. With a rush a large body sprang from the reeds. Had the pirates ambushed me? I almost cried out, but it was only one of the shore's big herons, and it settled down again with a sleepy croak.

My heart pounding, I listened yet again before taking a step. I heard only the buzz and whine of mosquitoes, which were rising and thickening the air around me. I put my back toward the pirates' lair and faced the island's northern shore, which I knew lay close to the Cuban mainland. Among the multitude of stars overhead, I picked one brighter than its neighbors—one I could "steer by" and so not lose my direction. I set out for whatever might lie on the far side of the swamp.

Almost at once my feet found a sort of pathway. I forgot my gnawing stomach and weak legs. I tried not to notice the buzzing insects which settled on every bare inch of my body. The ground under my feet seemed to consist of thick moss covered with a coarse grass. It was far from solid but it bore my weight. I encouraged myself, "I should cover a good distance before sunup." I hastened my step.

Without warning the crust of grass broke under my feet. I pitched forward … black ooze closed over my head. Frantically I fought my way through oily and scummy water. I spat out the mouthful I had not swallowed, and felt my stomach knot. I gagged on the fetid gas which rose from the disturbed water and its decaying plants. Then my feet were on comparatively firm bottom. I waded forward through the ooze, lost my footing, swam a few strokes, then waded again. The distance across the swamp hole was only a few yards, but movement was difficult, while the stench smothered and sickened me. I grew dizzy and faint.

The far edge of the hole was rimmed with stunted trees and bushes. Twice I caught hold of a branch to pull myself out. Twice the branch broke in my hand and I fell back into stinking mud. Then my hand grabbed some tough woody vines. Those seemed stronger than the half-drowned bushes, and with their help I struggled to ground that would bear my weight, inching forward with great care.

Again I had to lie face down and gasp for breath.

"To drown in a stinking mud hole will be as bad as being stabbed to death," I moaned to myself.

When I lifted my head, my ears caught the sea's soft wash along the cove shore. A few seconds passed while I tried to understand why this sound *should* bring me to my feet. Oh yes! It meant I was still within easy reach of my enemies. I heaved myself up.

I had learned a lesson. Like the familiar savannahs near home, this one had patches—islands we call them—of fairly solid ground surrounded by stagnant water under clogging weeds.

I broke a limb from a low tree and used it to feel my way forward. The moon was only a thin sliver in the western sky but there was starlight and, by straining my eyes through the darkness, I often caught an oily gleam that betrayed a water hole. Now and then the reflection of a star from a black surface warned me. Sometimes gurgling and squelching noises as I moved announced water ahead.

Some channels were narrow enough to jump across, although there was no telling what my feet would find on landing. When the ground broke under my sudden weight, I floundered through mud and a tangle of clutching vines until I could pull myself out and walk again.

Sometimes I could work my way around the darksome water holes, but then I had to find my star carefully and fix my course again. It would be all too easy to wander in a circle, exhausting myself and getting nowhere. Occasionally there was nothing for it but to plunge into the hateful black ooze and fight my way, splashing, wading, swimming—if it could be called swimming in such stuff—to the other side.

If I shrank from these ventures, I reminded myself of Dennis, of my slain friends, and I remembered the look in Jim Tyler's eyes. In that dismal swamp, in the blackness of night, driven almost crazy by the ravenous mosquitoes, I clung to the belief that Jim had kept fighting so that I might escape. I felt that every foot I gained pleased him.

Toward dawn I became light-headed and kept moving less by thought and bodily strength than by doggedness and habit. Before the eastern sky greyed I was twice forced to lie flat in the wet moss and wait for my strength to return before I could get to my feet and stagger on. I was losing the power to judge and pick my steps; instead I was stumbling and sprawling through the darkness, believing that the swamp would never end.

By dawn's first light I had gained higher ground, but I was now beset by scrub pine and thorny bushes. Spiny vines tore my bare feet and my almost naked body—my few remaining rags were little protection. I tried to cover my arms with one arm or the other as I went on, fearing I might be blinded by the needle-sharp thorns. In places the bushes were so matted that I could scarcely force my way through them.

The thin moon and my guiding star were gone from the sky when I caught a pale gleam from open water and knew I was near the island's inner shore.

I panted triumphantly, "Dennis will never believe I crossed the island. He thinks the swamp is a sure deathtrap." So it might well have been.

9
Escape

I broke out of the bush onto a sandy spit. The clean sea lapped along the shore, and the sweet dawn breeze rustled and sighed in the bushtops. The strengthening light disclosed that here the island and the Cuban mainland bulged toward each other. Not more than a half mile of water separated them. As far as I could see in either direction, nothing moved along the mainland beach. Not even a fisherman's hut showed among the palms. No hull or sail appeared between me and the seaward-thrusting Cape San Antonio to the westward.

I turned around. The wooded point hiding the pirate resort looked disappointingly near, for I thought I had covered interminable miles during the night. The yawl was nowhere in sight. I could see no splash of color, no flash of cutlass or knife in the rising sun—nothing to suggest that the pirates were again searching for me.

I reminded myself, "They are a lazy crew—no doubt still snoring in their blankets. But later—there's no telling what the day will bring."

I decided my only chance of final escape was to swim to the mainland shore and make my way toward Cape San Antonio. Perhaps the curving coastline hid a friendly village, or a fisherman who would take me to an official.

Ordinarily a half-mile swim would not have daunted me, but I had had an exhausting night. I had eaten nothing since yesterday noon, and then little enough, for our captors had always given us only so much as would keep our strength up to the level the work demanded. A great weariness lay upon me, body and spirit. I sat on the sand and watched the water gain color as the sun rose. I thought of the dawn, six mornings before, that had revealed the approaching yawl, and for all that had come about since. Salt tears stung my scratched face. There was no one to see them, and I felt them gradually ease the tight pain across my chest.

"Well, this won't buy the child a frock, nor

mend the old one," I scolded myself aloud. It was my busy mother's favorite saying, whenever she found herself pausing between tasks. The memory of my mother and my determination to see her again, brought me to my feet—then to the edge of the water.

I gathered my courage and struck out for the opposite shore. Terror found me again when, halfway across the channel, a shark's fin rose out of the water ahead of me. I should not have been surprised, but the thought of danger from these man-killers had not entered my mind. Now the dorsal fin knifing through the water was too much to face. I turned, thinking to regain the safety of the shore I had left. Two fins were breaking behind me! Panic-stricken, I thrashed about wildly.

Shipmates of later voyages tell me this was the best thing I could have done, since noise and commotion often keep sharks away. Also I have heard that sharks are least voracious at dawn. These may have been part of a well-fed school, bound for some definite spot and using the set of the channel's tide to their advantage. They paid no attention to me, although the water, both before and behind me, was briefly alive with their cruising fins.

When I reached the opposite shore, I staggered out of the water and, kneeling on the sand, I thanked God for my deliverance—from the murderers, from the swamp and from the sharks.

As I rose from my knees I saw a dead fish at the water's edge. It was far from fresh, but some of it was edible and my hunger outweighed my distaste. I devoured all I judged would not prove poisonous. High above me as I ate, a Man-o'-War bird had been hanging, its great wings motionless against the sky. I tossed the fish with its shreds of spoiling meat up and over the blue-green water. In a flash the black bird had hurled down, with half-closed wings and folded scissor-tail, had swooped and was swiftly mounting with the white bone hanging from its hooked grey beak. I doubted if the huge bird had been really hungry, yet it somehow pleased me that another living thing had shared my meal.

Above the tide line lay a dried Portuguese man-of-war, and a few feet off shore a live jellyfish of the same species trailed its long purple stingers.

The water revealed nothing else, and I moved back from the open beach. I began to walk along, staying near enough to the shore that I could sight any possible sail, but keeping always hidden from seaward. I had begun to hope that with the *Vernon* stripped and her crew disposed of, the pirates might sail back to Cienfuegos, ready to dupe another victim. But fear of the bloodstained ruffians never left me. I would take no chances. So, in case the yawl might cruise this coast, I made my painful way through low cactus and mats of guinea-grass. Again flies and mosquitoes descended like a curse upon me.

Silence lay heavily over the world. The sun climbed in a cloudless sky and I felt as if a hammer clanged in my uncovered head. The air grew oppressive.

After a time, despite my fear of being seen, I returned to the beach. But the lapping wavelets were too warm to comfort my torn feet, and the sea's blue glitter stabbed through my half-closed eyes. My stomach knotted upon its emptiness. I began to reel from heat and hunger, but fear of pursuit and the hope of a rescuing sail, kept me moving with numb persistence.

When the afternoon was wearing away, I came to a broken ridge of rock running out into the sea. Narrow pools of shadow lay at the foot of the larger boulders, promising some refuge from the sun. I moved toward them, limp and weak-legged. Then I saw the black mouth of a small cave among the rocks.

This was a welcome sight, but I warned myself, "Don't stop now. You must keep the distance you have gained on Dennis."

I turned and scanned the beach behind me. It held no sign of life. "I will rest long enough to ease my feet and aching head—no longer," I promised myself.

I pulled branches from a bush and, crawling inside the cave, placed them to hide the opening from anyone who might pass by.

As my burning eyes adjusted to the cave's dim light, I saw a rockface glistening with moisture. I licked it dry with my swollen tongue, and it cooled my mouth though it could not lessen my thirst.

After the heat outside, the cave felt chilly. Although my head was on fire, I shivered as I lay down upon the sandy floor. I thought I was again beside the front gate at home, with John MacLeod stamping his feet on the snowy road, while I said goodbye to my mother and sisters. Since I was determined to follow the sea, we were grateful—there at the gate—that John had found me a berth under him and that he was taking me with him to join our vessel.

My sisters were snivelling, while mother fumbled for her apron corner under her shawl fringe. (To tell the truth, my own eyes could have used a dab or two with an apron.) John said kindly, "Now, don't you fret Mrs. Peach, I'll take good care of Ben."

I moaned and became aware of my present surroundings. "Poor John," I thought. "How could he keep his promise? And now he's gone."

My aching legs and the cave's coolness again took me back to that snowy morning, when I was striving to place my new seaboots in John's wide-spaced footprints, as I followed him through the snowdrifts to the sloop to take us to Halifax.

Then I fell into a defenceless sleep.

10
Taking a Chance

When I awakened it was still broad daylight outside the cave. But the sun had somehow swung back from the western sky where I had last seen it and was high in the east. I thought I spoke but my parched throat and swollen lips probably uttered no sound. "The sun doesn't do that! Where am I?"

Memory gradually repeated the events of the past days. I realized I had slept away an afternoon, a night and some of the next morning.

"I can't face that lashing sun again," I moaned, and turned toward the cave's dark wall. As I moved a fiery pain ran through every joint, and nausea—from hunger and sunstroke—swept over me. "It would be easier just to lie here and wait my end," I said to myself.

A new sound—the roar of breaking seas—brought me out of my self-pity. It was the heaviest surf I had heard along the Cuban coast, and told

me a great storm must have passed while I slept,
too exhausted, or too delirious, to be sure of
nature's anger. Now I saw that the sky was a deep
and clean-washed blue. The thought of the cool
northerly wind, which had no doubt followed the
storm, brought me to my feet.

Only then did I realize just what a sorry state I
was in. Every muscle was as stiff and sore as if I
had been brutally beaten. My feet were so swollen,
and so lacerated by thorns, that I could scarcely
bear my weight upon them. Each bite and scratch
on my face and arms was now a festering welt. My
body was little better off, for my shirt was only a
ragged band across my shoulders. My stomach
growled; my head throbbed.

I limped to the rock at the back of the cave and
licked its blessed moisture. From the cave's mouth
I peered carefully about before venturing forth.
Surf was pounding in to break in smothering foam
along the beach. Beyond that, the blue ocean rolled
away to the horizon.

Far out at sea, a ship in full sail, a tower of white
above a thin line of black hull, went slowly
downwind. I might have reproached myself for
sleeping and so missed a chance of being rescued,
but plainly this ship had never been within many,

many miles of me. There was no other sail. I began to wonder if this coast was known to be pirate-infested, and was shunned by all but ignorant crews like the *Vernon's*.

My empty stomach rumbled. "Perhaps a fish has been washed up by the storm," I thought hopefully.

As I stepped into the sunlight, the night's havoc became evident. Snapped limbs and broken fronds lay where the wind had flung them. Here and there whole trees had been uprooted and flattened. I picked up a pine branch and, using it as a cane, began a painful hobble toward the water.

I managed to climb over the ridge of rocks which had formed my cave, and to make some progress along the shore on the other side. Suddenly a bird alighted on a branch just ahead of me. It was a little larger than a robin and looked something like a pigeon, but size and appearance did not matter. Soreness forgotten, I drew back my arm and hurled my cane.

The bird fell to the ground and did not move. I ran awkwardly to pick it up. Then I sat down and ate—scarcely taking time to tear the feathers from the meat, I sucked the warm blood and crunched the bones. "Like our tabby-cat with a sparrow," I thought. I was even making a growling cat-like purr, deep in my throat, as I ate. Ordinarily, I could not have forced myself to taste raw meat, but I doubt if I would have waited to cook that meal, even if I had the means of starting a fire.

The little bird made a new person of me. The aches left my arms and legs. My head cleared, and I could soon move more freely and strongly. I could rejoice that the sky was a high deep blue, that the sea danced and sparkled, and that running waves were tossing white foam along the sand. The fresh breeze had blown away yesterday's sultriness—along with some of my grief for my dead shipmates and some of my fear for their killers.

I decided against skulking among the underbrush or dodging between palm trunks. Instead, I walked openly along the beach, keeping a sharp lookout for a sail. "Around the next point," I heartened myself—then "around the next." But I rounded many of the small capes only to find the ocean still empty.

Then I saw in the near distance a headland higher and wider than those I had been passing. It shut from view a wide expanse of sea that would be visible from its crest. I hurried toward it, feeling a strange certainty that its far side would disclose something of promise.

My bruised feet and weak legs made the rough ascent to the headland's top far from easy, and I was breathless when I finished the climb. I tasted bitter disappointment. It seemed unfair that the offshore reaches should *still* be deserted. I dropped my eyes from the far view—and there, just beyond the line of breakers, glided a schooner! My heart gave a happy leap—then sank. I dropped flat on my stomach, hoping I had not been too boldly outlined against the sky, and that the schooner's crew had not been keeping too careful a watch to leeward, for this low rakish craft was no honest cargo carrier. It fitted descriptions I had heard of the swift pirate schooners. "Please, God, not another Dennis," I prayed.

During several minutes of despair, I barely raised my head from the ground, while I watched the graceful vessel. Then I was talking to myself, "Even if I was plain against the skyline, these marauders have no spite against me. They could see I am helpless and have nothing worth taking. They wouldn't put a boat and crew ashore just to hunt down a single ragged seaman."

Then another thought struck me. "Unless this

whole coast is under the rule of freebooters and strangers are not allowed to leave and tell what they've seen."

Again I watched the schooner with her lovely lines and gently rounding sails. "She is flying no flag, but I guess most pirates don't hoist their black ensigns." I laughed bitterly as I thought, "Some pretend to be government revenue boats! Still, she has a smart appearance. Such a trim ship couldn't belong to men like Dennis and his band. What a slovenly mess they made of the Vernon. Even their yawl is scuffy and in need of caulking."

Pressed flat to the ground and well-hidden, I continued to study the stranger. I looked once more over the vast and empty ocean. Soberly I weighed my chances of keeping alive until I could reach some village. These chances seemed far less rosy than they had a few hours before. If pirates controlled the coast, some buccaneer band could capture me *whenever* I showed myself. It might as well be today. I decided to throw myself upon the mercy of this schooner's master.

It was a relief to be free of the need to hide. I slipped and slid down the side of the headland and ran to the water's edge. The schooner was drawing abreast of me, but standing farther offshore. Suppose I had taken too long to make up my mind! I stripped off the few rags of my shirt and waved them aloft on a broken stick.

My signal was seen on the schooner, for a boat was lowered almost at once. With pounding heart I watched it manned, saw the oars take the water and the boat head toward me. But when it was within two hundred feet of the shore, the rowers stopped and leaned upon their oars. The surf was not heavy enough to prevent a landing on the even beach. Why didn't they come in? The man in the stern rose to his feet and hailed me—in Spanish I realized, disappointed. I had lost faith in men who spoke Spanish. But what else could I expect to hear along the Cuban coast?

In return I shouted, "Ahoy! Ahoy!" My voice was so thin and squeaky I doubted it would carry even the short distance.

The second hail came in broken English, and asked what I wanted.

"I want to come aboard," I yelled, pointing to myself and then to the schooner, to make my meaning clear.

The man in the stern consulted the others. The

bow oarsman stood up and peered under his palm at me, then all along the shore and at the trees behind me. This caution seemed a bit ridiculous.

"They're certainly not *bold* pirates," I told myself impatiently. "Even if they can't tell how weak and sore I am, they are still five to one."

The man in command of the boat—who I took to be the mate, as he proved to be—then shouted and gestured. "Swim off to us. We will pick you up."

Now it was my turn to hesitate. The rolling surf would not stop me, but I thought glumly how easy it would be for them to crack my skull with an oar as I came alongside—or to fill my body with bullets and let it sink. By showing myself to them, I had put myself at their mercy, since they could readily hunt me down ashore, if they wished to.

I caught hold of my courage. This time it was all or nothing. "I guess I should have been born a seal since I spend so much time in the water," I said aloud as I waded into the breakers. I dove through the next sea and started swimming toward the waiting boat.

No oar-handle or pistol-shot greeted me. As I reached to grasp the gunwale, I heard the surprised comment, *"El muchacho!"*—"a boy!" Strong hands seized mine and pulled me into the boat. I must have been a sorrowful sight. I did not need to understand Spanish to hear the pity and concern in the exclamations at my appearance. These men could not be pirates!

I began to tell them some of my story. When I said "red" and showed with my hands how Dennis' beard spread across his chest, they exchanged glances. The mate pulled me down upon a thwart, the oars ran swiftly out, and we headed back toward the schooner, now bearing down on us with most of the breeze spilled from her sails.

In difficult English the mate explained that his captain, *El capitan*, had ordered him not to approach too near the shore in answer to my signal. He suspected pirates had set up an ambush, and had sent me to the water's edge to decoy the boat within gunshot. The mate assured me that, had they known … they were most sorry.…

None of that mattered now, I told him with a wave of my hands. I thanked him again for coming to my aid. Secretly, I could scarcely believe that taking a desperate risk had led to my rescue.

11

Back to the Anchorage

It was mid afternoon when we drew alongside the schooner and I saw she was the *Fauro* of Havana.

Once aboard, the mate lead me aft to the captain, a middle-aged man with a neat black beard and the olive skin I had come to think of as Spanish. His brown eyes were kind as they looked down at my torn feet, my ribs—which stood out "fit to be counted"—my burned and scratched face, my matted hair, and my rags of breeches.

The mate spoke to him at some length, with gestures toward me and toward the shore, but I recognized none of his words.

When the mate had been dismissed, the captain introduced himself, "Antonio Peloso, master of the *Fauro*."

"Benjamin Peach, seaman, sir, of the brigantine *Vernon*, Halifax." Then I burst out, "I'm glad you

speak English Captain. I'm frightened of Spanish
… I mean, sir, I know only a word or two, and the
pirates…." I floundered on.

Captain Peloso smiled. I soon saw that along
with his English, he had a way of making his
meaning clear by his smile, a twist of his mouth,
and especially by his slender brown hands. "Come
with me to my cabin," he said. "We have matters
to talk over."

In his quarters a steward brought me a small
tray of food and wine. I fell upon it like the starving
animal I was. Not a crumb or a drop remained
before I apologized for my greed.

Polite Captain Peloso waved my words aside. "I
ordered small servings," he explained. "You had
been long without food, I did not wish you to
overeat and harm yourself."

I said I knew this was the proper thing for him
to have done, but I was still….

"There will be more soon," he assured me with
an understanding smile. "But first we must see to
those cuts and sores." Like most shipmasters,
Captain Peloso had gained some medical skill. He
set about cleaning the worst of my festered
scratches, and applying salves. "You are young

and healthy. These will heal quickly," he told me. "And now, if you are not too weary, I should like to hear your story."

I recounted the whole sad tale, beginning with our dealings with Mr. David of Cienfuegos. I explained the pirates pretence of being revenue men to lull our suspicions, and how the unarmed *Vernon* had been captured and plundered. I told how John MacLeod and George MacKay had been left at the pirates' haunt to be slain by their guards— how the rest of us had been taken on the pretended search for ballast. But when I tried to tell him of the Captain's murder, of Jim's ghastly wounds and his pleading eyes upon me, it was too much. I was no longer seaman Ben Peach, but a boy shaken and grieved at the death of friends—a boy heartsick with the knowledge that such savage evil existed in what had seemed a kindly world.

Now that I found kindness again—I broke down. Captain Peloso turned his back and studied a chart until I regained control of myself. I think he guessed I was no cry-baby, but that my spirit and strength had been strained to the breaking point. Perhaps he felt I needed to release the emotions that had been tearing me during my captivity and escape; fear and hatred, pity and helpless rage, loneliness and despair. He plainly understood that any words of sympathy at that time would have shattered me completely. He waited until I began, then turned around and listened as if there had been no interruption in my account.

When I had finished he said kindly, "Nothing can change the sad tale you have told me, but perhaps we can give your story a better ending."

He then told me, "A year ago the Spanish government of Cuba gave me command of this swift *Fauro*, with her fifteen man crew, and sent me to hunt down buccaneer bands along the coast." Proudly, he said, "The *Fauro* has done good work, but I am resolved to rid Cuba's shores of the last pirates—those scum of the plantations and ports! For some time stories have been reaching Havana about raiders off Cape San Antonio. We knew there must be a nest of them somewhere along this coast. We also heard they were under Captain Dennis. Last month *el almirante*—the admiral—summoned me to Havana. He ordered me to destroy this band before there is more serious trouble—for if one ruffian succeeds in mocking the authorities, will not others follow his example?"

I agreed that this seemed likely.

Captain Peloso stroked his beard. "Now you

tell me this Captain Dennis is really the merchant David, of Cienfuegos?"

"Yes, sir."

He went on, "I was cruising between Cape San Antonio and Cienfuegos, seeking Dennis and his outlaws, at the very time they captured your brigantine. But there are many islands and hidden coves on this shore." He made a gesture of fruitless searching. "I sighted no suspicious craft. True, I was looking for a schooner or a sloop. But a yawl— yes, I see how that would best suit these sea-robbers who dodge in and out of hiding."

After a moment's thought he continued, "If I could catch Dennis and his men at their rendevous, or find evidence there against them...." He looked at me sharply. "But I do not know their headquarters. I might cruise up and down for weeks and not discover it." I knew and dreaded what was coming. "Ben, if you will help me, we can soon have your shipmates' murderers in irons. Can you pilot the *Fauro* into the anchorage?"

I would rather have given my right arm than return to that scene of brutality and heartbreak. I might have armed friends with me, yet my terror of Dennis was so great that I felt nothing could save me from him if he found me still alive. Then I thought, "If I do as the captain asks, I may save other seamen from the fate of the *Vernon's* crew."

I answered as resolutely as I could. "I will recognize the island. I remember the entrance and the channel into the anchorage. I don't think I'll ever forget *anything* about that horrible spot."

He shook my hand warmly. "But you must get some rest, and some more food. The mate will bring you clothes and fix you a hammock forward. The wind is not fair and it will take time to reach the island. You will be wakened when needed."

The day was fading when the mate shook me awake. Though still somewhat stiff and sore, I felt much stronger as I slid from the hammock and followed the mate aft to where Captain Peloso stood studying the shore off our larboard bow. He lowered his telescope and spoke to me, "I believe that island ahead is the one we want."

"It is, sir."

"But night is almost here. We must anchor and await the morning."

"We *need* not, Captain. Just there," I pointed to a break in the trees, "the channel swings eastward past a wide beach, then around the next point to the mouth of the anchorage. There are no rocks to fear, for the shores are all sandy. If the schooner should take bottom on a sand bar, the flood will lift her before midnight. If we were already in place, we could surprise Dennis at first light."

"Mmm," he said, still considering the shore, "the wind is dropping with the sun."

I admitted that. "But, sir, when the *Vernon* lost the wind, Dennis made our crew tow her in by small-boat."

"We have sweeps," he mused. I remembered hearing that the low West Indian schooners were fitted with long oars and made much use of them. "We will try our sweeps when the winds fails us," Captain Peloso decided.

I stood aft by the captain, who translated my directions into Spanish for the helmsman and crew. The *Fauro* ghosted along, found the channel and had clear water under her keel. I peered into the deepening dusk and picked out familiar landmarks. Actually no great skill was needed in piloting the schooner, for only the island's trees had hidden the pirate's haunt. The entrance was fairly wide, the channel easily followed and there were no reefs to threaten a shallow-draught vessel like the *Fauro*.

Before long the slack sails were lowered, the sweeps manned and extra bow lookouts posted. By midnight we had swung around the last bend and the sweeps had been stowed. In the anchorage we showed no lights and kept the greatest silence. The barefoot crew moved almost without a sound and they lowered anchors with no more splash than a jumping fish might make. The *Fauro's* hull was black against the black shore. The same trees that had hidden the *Vernon's* masts now swallowed the *Fauro's*; from the shore there would be no betraying lines across the stars.

So, here I was, back in the horseshoe cove where the stripped *Vernon* lay—and where John and George lay buried in the sand, or deep under the quiet water, I thought sadly.

A red glow showed through the palm trunks, from the goods-yard where, as I told the captain, the buccaneers cooked their meals and lounged about.

"Good," he murmured, "I was afraid they might have slipped away, to Cienfuegos. Now, if only they don't suspect...."

"I don't believe the idea that their hiding-place could be discovered ever entered their heads," I told him. "They kept some watch when they thought we might try to escape. There's no need for that now." In spite of myself, my voice thickened, as I remembered how the rogues had ridded themselves of the task of guarding prisoners.

"Don't grieve." The captain put a kind hand on my shoulder. "The cook will give you some food. Then try to sleep again. We shall be early about. And I expect a busy day. *Buenos noctes*—goodnight—Ben."

"*Buenos noctes*, Captain Peloso," I replied warmly in my best Spanish—and my Nova Scotia accent.

12
The Black Roger

I wakened as the first shafts of morning light were slanting between the palms. Gradually I remembered where I was, and why. The captain's voice told me he was already on deck and giving orders to his men. Then I saw him. My heart knotted in frantic fear as I thought, "The *Fauro is* a pirate craft just as I suspected when I first sighted her!" Captain Peloso now wore a gaudy coat and a swinging cutlass; his beard was rumpled, his brimmed cap crushed and askew. His pistol belted men all had a swashbuckling air. Two of them were hoisting a signal-flag on the foremast … a signal? A breath of air fluttered the folds—*Black Roger.*

I sprang wildly from my hammock with the angle of leaping into the sea once again to save myself. But Captain Peloso, seeing me awake, beckoned me to him. I went, telling myself that his treachery was the hardest blow of all.

"I'm going ashore now," he said, "with two of my best men. Two are not enough to arouse suspicion. I hope to entice Dennis and his band aboard the *Fauro*. Here we can overpower them more easily than on land—and with less danger to my men. I shall tell him that I am one of the free-booting brotherhood and that I learned of a prize— a French ship, with a general cargo for Martinico, that has been driven off course and is making way toward the Yucatan Strait and Cape San Antonio. It is a rich prize but too large, I shall say, for me and my crew alone. By combining forces...."

I nodded my understanding, thoroughly ashamed of my fright and lack of faith.

"I shall ask him and his men to come aboard to make plans. If that does not bring them, I mean to use you as bait. I shall tell Dennis I have his escaped prisoner and that he has only to come aboard to claim you."

"But," I argued, "with only two men and yourself ashore, you'll be greatly outnumbered. If Dennis should suspect you, he will kill you."

"If my plan fails, and fighting starts ... if my men and I cannot get back to the *Fauro*, the mate has orders to clear at once for Havana. He will report to the authorities there. Have no fear, Ben, Dennis will not recapture you." Then, seeing that my concern was for him, he added, "Nor do I intend him to capture me." He climbed down into the waiting boat.

You may be sure I never stirred from my place at the *Fauro's* rail, nor took my eyes from Captain Peloso as the boat was rowed in toward the landing. It was the same landing I had known, yet something was different. The rising sun disclosed a blackened hull at the water's edge. The *Vernon* had been burned. The sands would bury her keel as it had buried the others whose charred timbers showed along the anchorage shore. No matter what happened now to her destroyers, she would never again breast the seas. But I could not let regret for the *Vernon* mist my eyes; they must be clear to watch what was taking place on the island.

We had dropped anchor a hundred yards offshore, but in the morning light everything looked much closer. I easily distinguished Dennis, by his size and by his red cap, as he walked toward the landing to meet his visitors. I could not be sure of the four men who followed him, but their identity was not important.

I watched Captain Peloso step ashore from the grounded boat, and Dennis come forward. I held my breath, half expecting the puff of smoke and the report of a pistol, or the flash of a blade. Instead, Dennis and his visitor fell at once to talking—talking and talking. Finally Captain Peloso turned back to the boat. His men pushed off and bent to their oars, but not until they were beyond musket reach from the shore did I draw a long breath.

As soon as Captain Peloso was back on the *Fauro*, he summoned me. "Ben, how many men did you say were in Dennis' band?"

"Six, sir, besides Dennis."

He nodded. "Then Dennis told the truth, I have good news for you! Your two shipmates are not dead—Dennis still holds them prisoners. I saw *four* men in the yard, besides those at the landing."

"John and George are alive!" My face and voice must have shown my joy.

Captain Peloso put his hand on my shoulder. "Alive, *now*," he said quietly. "I pray we are in time to save them. We must use great secrecy. If the pirates suspect why we are here, they will murder the captives before we can rescue them."

He told me the band had been puzzled and alarmed by the unexpected sight of the *Fauro*, for they had thought the anchorage unknown, even to other buccaneers. But Dennis' mistrust had apparently been laid to rest by the captain in his role of pirate, and by his own greed. He had been eager to join with his new fellow-raider in the capture of the rich prize. "Though I think he is scheming how he can use us to get the plunder, then snatch it from us," the captain said. "Perhaps it's all the better to have his mind working hard on this," he added.

Before he left Dennis, Captain Peloso had asked, as if it were of no great interest, "Have you lost a man lately? I picked up a young seaman on our way down the coast."

Dennis had cursed young Ben Peach. "From the brigantine we took a week ago," he explained, nodding toward the *Vernon's* hull. "He jumped out of our yawl. I thought we'd settled his hash with our pistols." He tossed his head toward the yard behind him. "I still have two of his shipmates—stubborn fools. I planned to finish them off today."

"No need to change your plans," Captain Peloso

had assured him. But the captain's mind had been busy about his own plans, for now he had to take into account the new fact that the lives of two Nova Scotians, as well as those of his own men, depended upon his course of action.

"The young seaman I mentioned is on my schooner. Why not," he suggested carelessly, "bring your men aboard the *Fauro* to have breakfast? We have a good cook in the galley. While our men are getting acquainted, you and I can decide how to capture the Frenchman, and where to sell her cargo. Then you can take your escaped man ashore—to join his friends, eh?" He laughed at his joke, knowing Dennis would expect another pirate to treat murder as lightly as he did himself.

Dennis had accepted the captain's invitation.

Though I did not learn their story until later, this is the place to tell what had been happening to the pirates' two prisoners.

13
The Fate of the *Vernon*

I still remember everything John and George told me: how they worried as they watched Captain Cunningham, Eddie, Jim and I launch the yawl and row it out of the anchorage. Dennis' roared orders came to them more and more faintly.

They wondered why they were left behind when either one of them could sweep better than young Ben or poor Captain Cunningham. They agreed that Dennis' talk of gathering ballast was just a lie—a thin one, to cover some other devilish scheme.

Daylight faded while the guards lolled in the palms' shadow, and the two friends kept an anxious watch for the yawl. As dusk descended they strained their ears for sounds of the returning boat, but night lay black upon the water before they caught the liquid whisper of oars. They heard the grate of keel on sand. Then something about the voices from the landing prepared them. They were not surprised when only Dennis and his men walked into the yard, but John groaned as he remembered with deep grief how he had promised my mother to look after me! George tried to comfort him, then both kept very quiet.

The returning pirates joined the guards about the fire which had been lighted as a smudge against the night insects. The flickering flames threw dark shadows across the evil faces. Juan Romero's earrings glinted, red as blood-stained blades. Dennis spoke to Daores, too quickly for John to catch any words. There was no need for words. The gesture of Dennis' hand across his throat, and Lopez's thrust with an imaginary sword, told the story. Slack-jawed Pablo grinned with relish, while the others guffawed. The captives braced themselves for attack.

Instead, Dennis ordered that the prisoners be given a few scraps of the *jerked* meat and *tortillas* upon which the guards had supped. They were again chained for the night.

As if murder made a cause for celebration, the pirates then broke open the *Vernon's* stores and fell to feasting. They gorged upon what hit their fancy and wastefully scattered other food across the sand. They broached a new puncheon of the *Vernon's* cargo, and began a wild carousel. This was the first drunken revel since the *Vernon's* capture, for Dennis had kept his crew under a tight rein until the brigantine had been unloaded and her crew rendered harmless. Apparently he now felt the time had come to give them more liberty.

John and George lay tense, expecting that at any moment one of the bloodthirsty villains would decide to spice the night's fun by killing the prisoners.

When his men had lost interest in food, Dennis rose with a shout, snatched a branch from the sand and lit it at the fire. The others hurried to do the same. Soon every man held a torch. With wild shouts they ran to the beach, flames streaming behind them. They swarmed up over the side of the forsaken *Vernon* and put their flares to her tinder-dry rigging and housing.

The night—sky and water and palm-trunked shore—was suddenly ablaze. Red, orange and yellow flames outlined the brigantine's bulwarks.

Fiery streaks ran up the masts and along the spars, forming crosses against the sky, and dimming the stars. Purple, blue and green tinged the tongues of flame that licked the deck and housings. The crackle of timbers and the hiss of steam, when raging fire met placid sea, came clearly to the captives' ears. Flaring tongues of leaping flames were mirrored in the water. Falling yards and bulwark planks crested waves that ran across the anchorage in garish rings. Sparks flew across the sky and were reflected from the black surface of the cove. The sight was heartbreaking and frightening, but wildly magnificent.

John had hated the thought that the pirates might re-rig the brigantine and use her to prey upon merchant ships. Piloting into the anchorage, he had told himself, "I'd rather see her, and all hands, at the bottom of the sea." To most seamen, a ship has honor and a life of its own. But what did the life and honor of ships or men mean to these outlaws? Less than nothing. Yet he had not dreamed that greedy pirates would wastefully destroy a nearly new vessel. Now, as he watched the *Vernon* burn, he told himself that they could never hope to sail her without betraying themselves. And she would not serve them as well as the yawl. Perhaps a swift death by fire was better than slowly rotting after all her crew had been killed.

The pirates left the blazing vessel and, wading ashore, came to her shore-boat, pulled up at the tideline. They applied their torches to it. Flames ran swiftly along low gunwales, then died. She had lain too long in the tide's reach to burn. As if mad for destruction, one way or another, the desperadoes ran for axes and smashed the boat to splinters where it lay.

For most of the night, while the *Vernon* burned, the pirates drank, shouted and sang. They even danced, reminding George and John of pictures of devils reeling beside the fires of hell. As flames weirdly lit the figures against the blank night, Dennis joined in the wild revelry, his tight red cape the color of blood where the firelight caught it.

Then, one by one, as drunkenness overcame them, the roisterers sprawled upon the sand. Only then did John and George close their eyes.

Next morning Dennis roused his men with savage kicks but, surprisingly, his ill-humor did not extend to his prisoners. When he addressed John, almost civilly, he asked if he could repair a boat, and John answered simply, "I am a shipwright."

Dennis then asked George if he were not the ship's carpenter on the *Vernon*, and when George said he had been, Dennis put both men to work making the yawl seaworthy. He ordered them to scrape the fouling weeds from its bottom, to patch garboards and cracked strakes. As the two set to work, Dennis ordered Daores to guard them but let them move about as was needed in their work.

Daores, plainly in an ugly temper from the previous night's debauchery, laid his naked cutlass on a broken cask beside him.

When the yawl was careened, the need for repairs was plain. Both men welcomed this work they knew and liked—it would take their minds off their dangerous plight.

A few yards downshore lay a loose pile of boards and planks, some of which looked serviceable. Mostly by signs, John asked Daores if this was to be used for repairs. The guard grunted assent and watched sullenly as his prisoner went to pick out suitable pieces.

The untidy pile held bits from many shipyards; English and American oaks, white cedar of Bermuda craft, mahogany used also in Bermuda, bits of hackmatack from New England and the Maritime provinces.

John told me as he rummaged and heaved boards and timbers to find what he needed that he found something that struck him motionless. He stood staring at a piece of wood in his hand. Weathered and faded, but still unmistakable, was the scrolled name-board of a Liverpool brig. Two years before, she had sailed on her maiden voyage—to the West Indies. She had not returned and was finally given up as "lost with all hands." This was a ship he had helped to build.

Memory carried him back to the shipyard where he had worked beside men he had known since boyhood. The air hummed with the blunt ring of mallets—wood on wood—and harsher clang of hammer on metal came from the forge of the ship's blacksmith. The fragrance of freshly sawn wood was strong and clean; even the smells of paint and pitch and oakum were pleasing.

He stood remembering the spring day the brig was launched. Wharves and shore had been crowded with men, women and children in holiday dress. He could hear again the happy shouts as she started down the ways, the roar as her stern struck water and sent swells rounding on either side to wash among the harborside rocks.

Every man of her crew had been his friend and neighbor. From his own bitter experience John guessed what must have happened before the name-board had been flung upon the heap of discarded wood. Were her seamen taken on a false search for ballast? Did their blood soak the sand or dye the sea? He thought of all the tragedies that lay behind the pieces of heaped wood, the rotting sails, the ship's gear and cordage that strewed the beach. "Dear Lord," he had asked with bowed head, "how many deaths? And how many more to come?"

He said he scarcely knew what he was doing as he moved back toward the yawl and tossed down his armful of gathered wood. Daores greeted him with broken English oaths and accused him of shirking work. John did not really hear his abuse.

Perhaps to Daores, the mate's silence seemed deliberate insolence. Perhaps in the bad temper following the night's orgy, he would have seized on any excuse to vent his vile temper. He snarled, swung about and snatched his cutlass. Before John could suspect any danger, he was slashed cruelly across the face.

George was working at the yawl's stern, but at Daores's snarl he spun about. He had tried to describe the horror he felt then, seeing John's cheek laid open to the bone. As Daores raised his wicked blade again, George leaped forward—a crazy thing to do, but in his rage he didn't care what happened as long as he could grapple with Daores and try to choke the life out of him.

But unexpectedly and even more swiftly than George, Dennis had moved. Steel flashed. Daores clutched his sword-arm as blood gushed out and Dennis, with drawn cutlass, roared, "I've warned you before, Francisco. When there's cutting to be done, I do it." With yellow eyes blazing he went on, "Disobey my orders once more, and I'll hack off both your arms."

For an instant Daores, his face twisted with pain and anger, looked as if he would spring at his leader. Dennis glared him down and Daores slunk away, cradling his bleeding arm.

The pirate chief stooped for a tuft of grass and

wiped his blade. He called Juan Romero to replace Daores as guard, then roughly ordered George to get water to clean John's wound, and to help him.

John needed help. Blood was streaming from his slashed face and he was close to fainting. George could do little to stop the bleeding or ease the pain. He tore pieces from his ragged shirt, to make crude bandages, but he had neither the skill nor the medicine to cope with such a wound. After a time he managed to staunch the flow of blood.

Juan Romero paid little attention to the prisoners while George was striving to apply his poor bandages, and John took the opportunity to tell what he had seen and why he had been too shaken to recognize the threat in Daores' curses.

14
Dennis' Proposition

As soon as John could stand, Dennis ordered both men back to work. In the late afternoon he strolled down to the yawl and waved Juan Romero out of earshot. He addressed his captives with the oily heartiness that had marked Mr. David. He said that he had always known they were strong and capable seamen, now he could see they were fine carpenters as well. Then he amazed them by saying that he needed crew with those skills and the ability to speak English. John could even be first mate.

John glanced toward Lopez, but with a scornful gesture, Dennis dismissed consideration of his fellow-pirate. He could see that the Nova Scotians were completely taken aback by this shift in the wind. "I'll give you time to think it over," he said with a great air of generosity. Plainly he had no doubt that both men would be glad to join his band.

John said later that he must have been out of his mind with pain, for he suggested to George that they might accept Dennis' offer, watching for the first chance of escape.

Not even for his wounded friend would George consider this, but he did leave it to John to decide for himself what he should do. George felt he would rather die right then than have any doings with such a bloody-handed outfit. He couldn't forget the murder of Captain Cunningham, a man he'd looked up to all his life ... or the other shipmates. Then he thought of me—so young, happy, friendly and helpful to all, he said; and they talked about the Liverpool brig and how John had just that day learned of her terrible fate. It seemed likely that if they joined with Dennis, the captain would use them, and their English, to lure other vessels into the same hellhole. John and George would be forced to kill more innocent men, making widows and orphans of their families at home.

The two agreed that the chance of escape from the pirate crew would be very slight and they groaned to think how helpless they were to bring the murderers to justice. At last, they put their faith in Providence to bring about the punishment, with or without help from them.

When the fading light put an end to work on the yard, Dennis came to them for his answer. George told me he gave it to him plain: "We know that you and your men murdered our captain and friends, and only God knows how many other seamen. We'd rather be killed right now than join you."

Dennis was dumbfounded to hear so plainly this refusal of a chance to live, and George repeated that they would not save their lives at the price of becoming murderous pirates.

The pirate's face darkened and his hand dropped to his pistol, but all he said was, "You'll die soon enough, if that's what you want." He stalked wrathfully away, muttering through his red beard.

That night the buccaneers sprawled about the fire. Some sat smoking, others threw dice. The fierce faces were now lit by the flames, now lost in the night's darkness. Rum flowed freely, but there was no such violence as had marked the previous night. Finally each fell asleep. Even Pablo, on guard, dozed where he sat, his pistol dropped on the sand beneath his hand.

Through the long hours, John tossed and turned from the pain of the slash on his face. Though he could not ease his friend's wound, George stayed awake to offer sympathy and companionship. In low voices the two discussed and discarded plans for escape. John considered that Daores wounded arm would hamper him while the others would probably think the odds of seven to two so great that they wouldn't expect any break for freedom—and at that time they were sleepy and unprepared. Could this be a chance?

But George pointed out that because they were in chains, they'd stand no chance even if they broke out of the yard; they could never get away over the sandy beach nor through the jungle. Even if they reached the yawl, John was so weak from loss of blood that they could not launch it.

They agreed there was no chance to escape, but they continued their low talk. Although neither put it into words, both men believed that because repairs to the yawl were nearly complete and they had turned down Dennis's offer, they would not live another night.

However, in the morning Dennis set them to work again. He wanted the yawl cleaned and painted, inside and out. The *Vernon's* looted stores provided paint and brushes, and the two friends tried to forget that these had been taken aboard so that the brigantine could be freshly painted when she re-entered Halifax Harbor after a successful voyage.

The day began with airlessness and the sea was glassy calm. In the sultry heat, work demanded great effort, while John was nearly driven to madness by the mosquitoes and flies which swarmed about his blood-soaked bandage and oozing wound. By afternoon short, hot gusts were tossing the palm leaves. These gusts soon rose to a driving wind that clashed the ragged fronds and the sun became a pale yellow disc burning through thin clouds. The weather-wise Nova Scotians sensed an approaching storm. Of the outlaws, only Dennis cast an occasional glance at darkening sea and sky, and even he seemed little concerned.

As the day was ending, Dennis came to inspect the completely repaired yawl, gleaming in her fresh paint. Again he offered the prisoners their lives as members of his gang. This time John put their refusal into words, as bluntly as before, and the pirate shouted that tomorrow they would die.

The wind continued to rise in tremendous squalls. By nightfall a hurricane was ripping across the island. Roaring winds bent the thrashing palm-tops and curved the bare trunks like bows. Branches snapped with the sound of sails tearing, and shredded fronds whipped into the darkness like canvas rags. The anchorage was churned into white hills that gleamed through the night. Rain fell in torrents.

The pirates sought shelter in the lee of the thick undergrowth at the yard's end, but left their chained captives to endure the storm's full violence. For a time the two friends thought swollen tide and raging seas might sweep over the island and put an end to captors and captives alike. Sand, carried by the howling wind, inflicted torture upon John's face. But the rain must have been cleansing, for in the morning the wound looked less angry. George then lost some of his unspoken fear that the untended injury might cause blood poisoning.

By dawn the center of the storm had passed. The wind then swung around and came clear and strong out of the north, cool enough to set the prisoners shivering until the sun rose to warm them.

The hurricane had granted another reprieve. Driven sand had scoured the yawl's fresh paint down to the bare planks, and Dennis set them to repainting. During the day he came several times to renew his offer. He could not believe men would throw away their lives, and the chance of plunder, for what he could only consider mere notions against robbery and murder. As night drew on and their attitude did not change, he became more and more enraged. In the end he stormed off shouting, "Then sleep well. This is your last night on earth."

These words were scarcely conducive to slumber or hope, but for some reason George felt almost at peace for the first time since he had watched the yawl carry away his captain and friends. When he and John were once more chained on the sand, and Pablo was out of hearing, he shared with John his new conviction that something would happen soon to save them again. John was doubtful that anything so wonderful would happen; they were no longer useful to Dennis, and he had heard Lopez and Juan talking. From what he could understand, the pirates were starting back to Cienfuegos very soon. And who would rescue the two prisoners? No one in all the world knew where they were.

Their sleep was broken and troubled, so that dawn came as a relief. Indeed it brought a brief upsurge of hope, for it disclosed a schooner lying at anchor a hundred yards off shore. But hope soon dwindled, as John noticed that the schooner was no cargo vessel with such rakish lines; it had carelessly approached rendezvous as if the crew knew the men ashore, and had nothing to fear from them.

Hope flared briefly as the new ship ran up a flag, but it was a Black Roger, and in pain and despair John turned his disfigured face to the ground.

To judge by their gestures and exclamations, Dennis and his men were puzzled by the schooner. The prisoners were forgotten in this new development.

John kept his face buried on his arm, but George told him of each movement as the schooner lowered a boat. Two men climbed into it, and one, a mate or the captain, took his place in the stern.

The boat cast off and headed for the landing; now Dennis beckoned Juan and Fernandez to him, and waved Daores and Pablo to watch the two prisoners. All the others fell in line behind Dennis, who strutted down to the landing, straightening his red cap and loosening his cutlass. The man who was in charge of the boat stepped ashore—a smallish man, wearing bright clothes—another freebooter, no doubt.

Despite his disappointment in the new arrivals, George continued to watch and report. "The new man and Dennis have lots to talk about. Now they're pointing at the schooner. Now Dennis is waving a hand toward us—or at the loot he has stored here. Perhaps this schooner carries away the pirates' plunder and disposes of it. More talk. Dennis is agreeing to *something*. Now the little man is stepping into his boat. It's heading back to the schooner. Dennis and his men seemed pleased. Some plot has been hatched!"

Dennis returned to where the open-mouthed Pablo and Daores, with his arm in a sling, stood sullenly on guard. Of the orders given these two, John could catch only *"Captain Peloso"* and *"desayuno"* (breakfast).

Then Dennis walked down the beach to where his men waited beside the yawl.

"Pablo and Daores appear none too happy at being left behind," George reported. "It looks as if Dennis and his men are off to enjoy breakfast with the newcomer and *his* crew. May it poison every last one of them!"

He turned to his friend, "But don't give up, John. I still have *that feeling*."

15
Friends Reunited

I could have danced on the *Fauro's* deck when Captain Peloso gave me the news that George and John were still alive. But, while the captain could understand my joy, he had other things on his mind.

"Now, Ben," he told me gravely, "Dennis and his men will be coming aboard shortly. They must not suspect that I am your friend. You had best be below, as if you are a prisoner ready to be passed over to the outlaws." Seeing the disappointment on my face, he relented. "Or you could be tied up on the foredeck."

"Tied," I begged, and held out my hands, "so I can see all that happens." One of the *Fauro's* crew came forward and roped my wrists.

The captain continued, "Dennis is leaving two of his band ashore to guard your friends. I could think of no way to change that without making him suspicious. I have fifteen men, so there is no doubt about our capturing the five pirates who come aboard. I am hoping the thoughts of breakfast will take them all below. Then we can trap them without bloodshed. But your friends' lives depend upon our overpowering *all* the pirates aboard, without alarming the two ashore. For if the guards suspect their comrades have been taken, they will kill the prisoners before they run away. What I plan is a gamble and the stakes are your friends' lives."

While I was being roped to a foremast cleat, Captain Peloso gave rapid orders to his men. Arms were laid out, hidden by the bulwark but within reach. The forward hatch was cleared and the door to the cabin companionway fastened back.

When Dennis and his four oarsmen pulled alongside, most of the *Fauro's* crew were lining the rail to welcome them. The red cap of the pirate chief, as he clambered over the schooner's side, was the first sight I had of my enemy. His men, all heavily armed as usual, followed him aboard.

His eyes found me at once. They lit up with malicious delight. "So we meet again, my fine swimmer," he said, and laughed his ugly laugh.

I hung my head, so that I wouldn't betray my joy at the success of Peloso's plan. But something about me alerted Dennis. I heard him actually sniff the air for danger, even as he wheeled toward the captain. His hand dropped to his cutlass and he opened his mouth to shout an order to his men. He was too late. Before a single man could cry out or draw a weapon, rough hands had closed over their mouths and were pinioning their arms. There was the briefest of scuffles. Peloso's men kept up a chorus of merry shouts and laughter while they were bundling the pirates below decks. Watchers or listeners ashore would see and hear nothing but the noisy mingling of two friendly crews.

The last pirate to disappear—dumped down the forward hatch like a sack of potatoes—was Dennis. In the tussle his cap had been pulled off. I could scarcely believe my eyes! Under the red cap, worn day and night, Captain Dennis of the flowing beard and matted chest was as bald as an egg! I remembered that as Mr. David he had never appeared without his sombrero. That bloodstained, heartless buccaneer was ashamed—not of murder—but of being hairless. When the *Fauro's* mate cut the ropes from my wrists, I was laughing as if I had taken leave of my senses.

Now that the tide of fortune had turned in our favor, even Dennis' red cap would serve in our friends' rescue. Though I did not understand the reason at the time, I saw Captain Peloso pick it up and replace his own brimmed hat with it.

Once the swift skirmish on deck was over, the captain ordered his boat brought to the *Fauro's* offshore side, out of sight of the men at the landing. He took four oarsmen and two other men who were ordered to crouch below the gunwales.

"Let me go with you," I begged, for I couldn't bear to stay idle aboard ship while the fate of George and John was being decided. "It might help if my friends recognize me and know we come to rescue them."

Captain Peloso yielded to my pleading. "But keep hidden in the bow until we are well ashore."

Crouched in the bow, I could see nothing ahead until our keel grated on the sand, and Captain Peloso and his men leaped to their feet. I was among them as they jumped ashore and began to run across the yard.

George told me later Pablo and Daores had watched the boat's approach uneasily. But the sight of their leader's red cap in the stern reassured them for a time. Daores must have been in pain from his wounded arm. This, along with Pablo's slow wits, may explain why they took no alarm until they saw us spring from the boat. Even then they stood for a few seconds, staring in amazement, before they ran for their muskets.

Perhaps Daores thought the schooner's crew had wiped out Dennis and his men, as a rival band, and now planned to seize the yard's stored plunder. (Daores would never have believed any nonsense about "Honor among thieves.") At any rate, the rescue now took an unexpected turn. Seeing themselves outnumbered, and realizing that something had happened to their comrades, the guards turned to their prisoners for help. They hurriedly freed John and George, and Daores thrust pistols into their hands.

"Shoot! For your lifes!" he urged them in broken English.

George could by now distinguish the figures running toward him. "John! That's not Dennis in the red cap. These men are all strangers ... except— oh thank God, John—except young Ben Peach!"

Captain Peloso was shouting and waving to them. "To the boat, the boat."

I added my cry. "It's me, John. This way, George. Run for the boat."

But the guards were making no attempt to stop or harm their prisoners. They were fleeing for the jungle wall behind them, dropping their hastily snatched muskets. Captain Peloso raised his pistol and fired—fired again. From behind me came other shots.

Pablo reeled and fell. But he got to his feet and plunged blindly into the matted growth at the end of the yard. The green wall closed behind him. When we searched we found drops of blood on the outer bushes, but no trail we could follow. Much later I often wakened in a cold sweat, having dreamed I was again being sucked down in one of the swamp's fetid water holes, bitten by flies and ripped by thorns. I would think then of Pablo's flight and what insects and thorny undergrowth must have done to his open wound. I could not picture him surviving to take up a raider's life again—although he may have done so, for no word of his fate ever reached us.

Daores ran awkwardly because of his bound arm. A shot brought him down before he reached the end of the yard. I saw him spin on his heel, clasp his thigh and fall to his knees. Almost immediately the *Fauro's* men had bound him and were half-carrying him to the boat.

I turned then to my shipmates who were standing in a daze of disbelief. Captain Peloso had given me some hope for my friends, but they had had no hint of my escape.

"You freckled-faced son-of-a-gun!" George said, and flung his arms around me.

John greeted me huskily, "We never expected to set eyes on you again, Ben."

My joy at our reunion was somewhat dampened when I had time to observe my friends. George, peeling from sunburn above a straggling black beard, was gaunt from little food and hard work. John's muscular frame was a mere skeleton of what it had been. But it was John's face that wrung my heart. His eyes were sunken, he was ghastly pale—even his tan had greyed and faded. What most drew and repelled my gaze was the frightful gash down the length of his left cheek. The sword had barely missed his eye. I had never seen torture, although never once did I hear John complain, and George told me that no word of what he was suffering had ever crossed the mate's lips.

There was no time then to ask or answer questions. After our useless attempt to track Pablo, we were quickly rowed to the *Fauro*, with the bound Daores in the boat's bottom. I found it enough to sit and feast my eyes upon the two men who had come back to me, as if from the dead.

Before we reached the schooner, we saw the Black Roger was being hauled down, having served its purpose. Once we were alongside, Daores was half-pushed, half-pulled onto the schooner's deck. Here Captain Peloso passed him into the hands of the cook, who succeeded in extracting the bullet from his thigh, and who dressed the gashed arm before the pirate was carried below to join his comrades.

From then on, only an occasional rumble of voices came from the forward hatch to remind us of our unwilling passengers.

Captain Peloso treated my friends with the same kindness that I had received. They were fed and supplied with clean clothing. The captain gave John a dark drink to ease the pain, then cleaned his wound and applied an ointment. Each man was allotted a hammock on the after-deck and told to sleep as long as he wished.

The *Fauro's* crew set about preparing to leave

the hidden anchorage. Sails were set, anchors raised and, on the ebb tide, the schooner moved seaward. I took my place beside the helmsman again, proud that out of the perils I had come through I had gained the knowledge that now enabled me to pilot the *Fauro* through the winding channel.

I said a silent goodbye to the *Vernon's* hull, desolate at tideline, and to this forlorn heap that had been our boat. The puncheons which had formed the *Vernon's* cargo stretched along one side of the goods-yard. When I mentioned them, Captain Peloso assured me that, once he had delivered his prisoners to the authorities, the puncheons would be collected, taken to Havana and held for their rightful owner. Owner? How faint and faraway Mr. Strachan of Halifax had become.

By next morning the pirate island (strange that I never heard its name, if it had one) had dropped below the skyline astern. Then we met head winds and were two days beating around the split Cape of San Antonio. It was during this time on the *Fauro*, while John's wound began to heal and we all regained strength and spirits, that we exchanged stories.

I told the others of that terrible afternoon when

we had rowed away in the yawl, and how my fear had been for *them*, left behind. "I don't think Jim or Eddy was expecting foul play in the yawl. I know I wasn't. Captain Cunningham may have been. I remember he had a tragic look, but I had become used to that...."

"Yes," John interrupted quietly. "Looking back, I believe he carried the foreknowledge of his death from the moment Dennis stepped over the brigantine's side and laughed that cruel, gloating laugh."

"He'll never laugh again at honest seamen," George reminded us. My heart, though no longer filled by fear and grief, could yield no slightest throb of pity for Dennis, nor any of his cutthroats.

16
Home—at Last

The rest of our story takes little telling, though the close of our unhappy voyage dragged on unendingly for the three survivors, filled as we were with a longing to be home.

The *Fauro* arrived at the mouth of Havana Harbor just as the sunset gun from Morro Castle denied entrance and departure to all shipping. Such cannon guard the approaches to many West Indian ports which have had a long history of night attacks from the sea. We anchored to await the sunrise gun.

The morning sun coppered the headland rocks and the heavy masonry of the fortresses on either side, as the *Fauro* sailed into the entrance passage. Havana's spacious harbor held ships from many countries, and a multitude of lighters were moving among them. The city, covering a rounded peninsula, was the largest I had ever seen. According to John it had five times as many people as in Halifax.

At home I had thought I would like to visit Havana, that port of which so many seamen spoke, but now I lacked the heart to appreciate its beauties.

Two crewmen were sent ashore in the *Fauro's* boat with messages to the port officials. The officials soon came on board, plainly delighted with Captain Peloso and the success of his latest cruise. The miserable pirates were transferred from the schooner's hold to a naval launch and taken to dungeon cells ashore.

It was right that these men should be imprisoned, but I could see no justice in the orders of the choleric Spanish Admiral when we appeared before him. We were to be locked up in the guardhouse until needed to testify at the pirates' trial. Popular Captain Peloso spoke on our behalf, but the Admiral's orders were carried out. We were well-fed and not ill-used in any way, but we all resented being under guard again.

Things changed on the third day when the British Consul, Mr. Tolme, had us released. From then on we had the best of treatment and lacked nothing.

We three had not a single coin among us, but the Consul assured us his government provided funds for seamen in distress. (I suspect some extras were paid for out of his own pocket.) He found us lodgings with a friendly family who spoke some English and during daylight hours we were free to go about the city as we wished.

Huge, flaming red flowers gave the city a festive look, while its old buildings and grill-windowed homes lent quaintness. No one went out during the midday heat, but in the mornings and afternoons we mingled with the brightly dressed, happy-looking crowds. At sunset we liked to visit the seawall where citizens strolled or sat on the long rampart to watch the orange and purple sunsets.

But the time passed slowly, while I wished impatiently, "Come day! Go day! God send the day that will see us homeward bound." I would have traded all Havana's flowers, fruits, beautiful beaches and gaudy colors for Halifax's rocky grey shores and fishy wharves. Yes, and I would have thrown in Halifax too, to be back in my mother's Liverpool cottage—a boy home from the sea.

Finally, the day of the trial arrived. All Havana

must have turned out to attend. I could scarcely recognize the pitiful creatures hauled into court. John and George identified the pirates, but I was the chief witness against them, for only I had seen and survived their orgy of murder. I could not bear to look at them long, but I was glad I had been forced to see them again—for the fear and hatred that had festered in my heart, burst like a bad boil and drained away.

I felt those wicked men should die, if their death might save innocent mariners. Yet a faintness came over me when Mr. Tolme translated the sentence passed upon them. "They are all to be shot on the mole in Havana Harbor. The head of Francis Dennis, alias David, is to be placed on the highest point off Cape San Antonio, near where piracy and murders were committed; the heads of the others are to be placed at various points about Havana Harbor as a warning against any would-be piracy."

Once the date of the trial had been set, Consul Tolme had secured our passage on a Halifax-bound brigantine. The day after judgement was passed down, we went aboard ship. Eighteen days later we arrived in Halifax after an uneventful voyage.

Our joy at homecoming could not help but be clouded by memories of those who had not returned with us.

News of our adventures had reached Halifax soon after Captain Peloso had brought us into Havana. In heavy black type, "Horrid Act of Piracy" and "Murder on the Spanish Main" headed the Halifax newspaper stories. These accounts had been copied from the New Orleans *Picayune*, which had received its news by letter from Havana.

The first naval vessel leaving Havana from Halifax had carried Consul Tolme's account to General Sir Colin Campbell, Lieutenant-Governor of Nova Scotia. He had ended his letter: "... merchant vessels ought always to have means of defending themselves, which was unfortunately not the case with the *Vernon*." (In spite of the Consul's advice and the *Vernon's* fate, I never heard of any Nova Scotian vessels being armed.)

I was pleased to learn that, soon after our story reached Halifax, fifty of that city's young men had called a meeting and resolved to send a gold medal and chain to Captain Antonio Peloso "as testimonial to his noble conduct in capturing the murderers of Captain Cunningham and in lasting remembrance of his service to our country and to people."

As to the three survivors: George MacKay shipped out on another voyage shortly after arriving in Halifax. He was lost at sea while still a young man. John MacLeod never completely recovered from the wound he suffered at the pirate's hands. I used to visit him when home between voyages. Although he was eager to hear— as I was to tell—of foreign ports and storms at sea, we seldom mentioned the *Vernon* or her crew. We kept those memories deep in our hearts.

I was young; I soon threw off the terrors I had known on my first West Indies cruise. The following spring I shipped on a barque bound for the Bahamas, and after that I made many a voyage down the Spanish Main. I always took pains to ask the port of destination before I signed on, so that I never had to put in at Cienfuegos again.

Although for a few years I heard stories of Nova Scotian vessels being chased by pirate craft, I must say I never again sighted so much as a suspicious-looking sail—which suited me fine!

Glossary

BARQUES Sailing ships with three masts.

BELAYING PINS Removable pins on the rails of ships, used for fastening rigging lines.

BOW-GUNWALE The reinforced top edge of the side of the bow of a ship. It is designed to make the side stronger and to provide support for **tholepins**.

BOWSPRIT or **WIDOW-MAKER** The bowsprit is a pole that juts out from the bow of a ship and is used to hold one corner of a triangular sail. Sailors were sent out on the bowsprit to furl or adjust a sail and some fell off and were drowned. Thus the bowsprit was often referred to as a "widow-maker" because it made widows of so many sailors' wives.

BRIGS or **BRIGANTINES** Square-rigged ships with two masts. The *Vernon* was a brigantine.

CAPSTAN A devise used by sailors to hoist the anchor.

CATSPAWS Light breezes that ruffle the water.

COAMING A raised edge around a hatch or opening in the deck of a ship. The coaming prevents water from running down below into the hold of the ship.

COMBERS Waves that roll over or break at the top. These are also called "breakers".

CROSSTREE Horizontal bar of wood near the ship's mast. A ship's boy, such as Ben Peach, would climb the mast and sit astride the crosstree as a look-out.

CUTWATER The front part of a ship's prow. It is the part of the ship that slices, or cuts, through the waves first.

DITTY BOX A small box used by sailors to store

sewing things and other odds-and-ends. Some sailors had ditty bags.

DOGFISH A small, voracious shark, hated by fishermen. They frequent waters off Nova Scotia.

FID A pointed wooden pin used to open strands of rope in splicing.

FLUKES The parts of an anchor that bite into or catch the ground.

FORECASTLE The sailors' quarters where they slept, located in the forward, or front, part of the ship.

FOWLING A light gun used for shooting wild birds. A ship such as the *Vernon* would probably have a fowling gun so that the crew could shoot birds to add variety to their diet. Most meat on board ships was dried and wild birds offered a tasty treat.

FULL-RIGGED A sailing ship, completely equipped with masts and sails.

GARBOARD The first plank of wood used in building a ship. The garboard is secured to the keel.

GIBBET CHAINS The gibbet was an upright post with a projecting arm at the top. The bodies of criminals, such as pirates, who had been executed were hung by chains from the gibbet arm as a warning to other seafarers.

HAWSER A large, stout rope, used for mooring or towing ships.

JERKED Meat cut into strips and dried in the sun. Most meat on board the *Vernon* was jerked.

KEDGE-ANCHOR A small anchor used to kedge, or haul a ship. The kedge-anchor is thrown and secured some distance from the ship. Then the sailors haul on the anchor chain, moving the ship slowly forward.

LALLYGAGGING Slang. Someone who lolls or hangs around annoying other people.

LARBOARD Left, or **port**, side of the ship when facing the bow.

LUGSAIL A four-cornered sail held by a yard that slants across the mast.

PACKET BOATS Small boats that carry mail, passengers and goods regularly on fixed routes. The English packet boats travelled between England and Halifax.

PALM A fitted leather with a thimble fixed in it that is strapped around the hand. The thimble is located on the ball of the thumb and is used by sailors to push a needle through sailcloth.

PAWLS A sheet (or rope) used for hauling in sails is pulled through the pawl. A catch stops the sheet from slipping out.

PEONS Spanish-American term for people who routinely do work requiring very little skill.

PINTLES Upright pins or bolts which allow another object to turn. They are similar to hinges.

PUNCHEONS Large casks containing rum.

REEF-POINTS Points on a sail that indicate how

far the sail may be reefed, or rolled up, during heavy weather.

SCHOONERS Ships with two or more masts and fore-and-aft sails.

SPYGLASS A small telescope.

STARB'D The right side of the ship when facing the bow.

STERN SHEETS Space at the stern of an open boat.

STRAKES Single planks of wood that make up the hull of a ship. Each strake runs from the bow of a ship to the stern and is made of one continuous piece of wood.

SWEEPS Long oars for rowing a boat in the sea. The pirates used their sweeps to poke the water when they were looking for Ben Peach.

TARRING Putting tar between the planks of wood, or strakes, to stop the hull from leaking.

THOLEPINS   Wooden pegs that hold oars in place. They are located at the top of the gunwales.

TORTILLAS Thin, flat bread, cooked on a heated stone.

WARPED   A ship that has been moved along a wharf by pulling on a rope tied to the wharf.

WINDLASS-BITT A windlass is a machine used to pull or lift cargo off a ship. The bitt restrains the windlass so that movement of the cargo may be controlled.

YAWED A sailing ship that has turned slightly off course is said to have "yawed". The *Vernon* yawed, or altered her course slightly because of the pull of the current.

997034

00268811
DARTMOUTH REGIONAL LIBRARY